"What are you thinking?"

"I was thinking that if you did want to take me to bed perhaps it might be a good thing," she said thoughtfully, and felt him tense against her.

"Would you say that again?" he demanded.

"I'm sure I don't have to."

"So why do you think it would be a good thing? From my own point of view it's a ravishing idea, of course, but—"

"I think it would give me closure."

"Closure?" Alasdair put an ungentle finger under her chin to raise her face to his. "What does that mean?"

Kate looked at him defiantly. "Meeting you again has revived old ghosts. Maybe going to bed with you would lay them for good."

The Dysarts

A family with a passion for life—and for love.

Welcome to the fifth story in THE DYSARTS saga,
by popular Presents® author Catherine George.
A few years have passed, and now Kate Dysart is
in her twenties and coming to terms with love
and relationships. When Alasdair Drummond
returns to her life, Kate finds herself at an
emotional impasse. Once Alasdair saw her
as a friend—now he says he wants her.
Only, Kate isn't about to succumb....

Come share in the trials and joys, the hopes and
dreams of the Dysart family, as they live their
lives with passion—and for love.

Catherine George

SWEET SURRENDER

The Dysarts

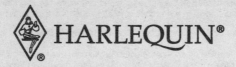
HARLEQUIN®

TORONTO • NEW YORK • LONDON
AMSTERDAM • PARIS • SYDNEY • HAMBURG
STOCKHOLM • ATHENS • TOKYO • MILAN • MADRID
PRAGUE • WARSAW • BUDAPEST • AUCKLAND

ISBN 0-373-12306-X

SWEET SURRENDER

First North American Publication 2003.

Visit us at www.eHarlequin.com

Printed in U.S.A.

CHAPTER ONE

KATE was about to dismiss her class of lively eight-year-olds for half-term, when the headmaster called her outside into the hall.

Bill Vincent eyed her hopefully. 'Can you do me an enormous favour, Kate?'

'Of course, if I can. What's the problem?'

'Could you possibly hang on with young Abby Cartwright for a while? Her father's on the phone from the hospital—'

Kate winced. 'Not the baby already?'

'Weeks early, hence the panic. Fortunately the grandparents were arriving today anyway. Abby's uncle is fetching them from Heathrow, and will collect her on the way back.'

'Which means Uncle's not likely to collect Abby any time soon, then,' she said, resigned.

'Afraid not. I've got a Consortium meeting, or I'd stay myself—'

'Better if I do it,' said Kate promptly. 'I'm her teacher, the one she knows best. She's new this term, and so shy she's finding it hard to make friends. I'll take her home with me.'

The Head smiled, relieved. 'Thanks a lot, Kate. Will you give Tim Cartwright the glad news? I'll look after your class.'

Kate picked up the phone in the office to reassure a distraught Tim Cartwright.

'I'm on a hospital payphone, Miss Dysart, so I'll be

5

brief,' he told her. 'Julia's desperately worried about Abby and wants me to go home, but I hate the thought of leaving her. Mr Vincent said you'll take care of Abby, but are you really prepared to do that until my brother-in-law arrives? He could be late.'

'No problem at all, Mr Cartwright,' said Kate soothingly. 'You stay with your wife and tell her not to worry. I'm taking Abby home with me. Laurel Cottage at the end of the village. But could you contact her uncle, please, and give him my phone number?' Kate waited as he made a note of it, cut short Tim Cartwright's fervent thanks and went back to her class to report to Bill Vincent that everything was sorted.

When the other children streamed out to join waiting parents Kate called Abby Cartwright from the window. The child turned quickly, her blue eyes anxious behind her spectacles, fine flaxen hair escaping from its bunches.

'Abby,' Kate said gently, 'your father won't be picking you up today. He's just taken your mother to the hospital to have the baby—'

'But he can't come yet, Miss Dysart, it's too soon!' said the child in alarm.

'You know it's a boy, then?' Kate smiled reassuringly. 'Don't worry. Baby brother's in a hurry, that's all. Your uncle's coming to collect you on the way back from the airport.'

'Then he's gone to fetch Grandma and Grandad,' said Abby with relief. Her face fell. 'But do I have to wait here at school until they come?'

'No. I'll take you home with me.'

After Kate had collected her belongings and surrendered the classroom to the caretaker who doubled as cleaner, she said goodbye to her colleagues and took

Abby out to her car. Because the village school was too short of space for a car park her elderly little runabout was outside in the village street, as usual, and as Kate approached it with Abby a man emerged from a sleek foreign vehicle parked a short distance away.

Kate stared in utter amazement, convinced for a moment that she was seeing things. But Alasdair Drummond, even taller than she remembered in a formal dark suit, was too solid a figure to be an apparition.

'Hello, Kate.' He strode towards her, hand outstretched, his smile familiar and self-confident.

Kate touched the hand briefly. 'This *is* a surprise, Alasdair. What on earth are you doing here?'

'I came to see you, Kate.'

He expected her to believe that?

When she made no response his eyes narrowed. 'I realise I should have got in touch first, but I've been to a funeral, so on impulse I came out this way afterwards on the chance of seeing you.'

Kate turned to the child beside her. 'I'll just pop you in my car, Abby, while I talk to this gentleman for a moment. Shan't be long.'

Kate fastened Abby into the passenger seat, closed the door and looked up at Alasdair Drummond, displaying none of the over-the-moon delight he'd obviously expected. At one time she would have given her soul to see him turn up out of the blue like this. But not for many a long year, and certainly not here, where they were attracting far too much attention from her departing colleagues.

'One of your pupils?' asked Alasdair.

'Yes.' Kate explained the situation briefly. 'So I'm afraid you've come out of your way for nothing—I can't even ask you to my place for a coffee.'

'I'd hoped for a lot more than coffee.' His eyes held hers. 'Take pity on an old friend, Kate, and have dinner with me tonight.'

He had to be joking!

'Sorry, Alasdair.' Not that she was, in the slightest. 'Even without the present complications I'm much too busy. I'm going home tomorrow for half-term—'

'I know. Your brother told me over lunch yesterday.'

Kate's eyes narrowed. 'You've seen *Adam*?'

'He's auctioning some furniture for me.'

And Adam hadn't seen fit to mention it?

Kate caught sight of Abby's anxious face through the car window. 'Look, I really must go.'

Alasdair caught her hand. 'I'll ring you later. Adam gave me your number.'

Less pleased with her brother by the minute, Kate detached her hand, said goodbye, got into her car, backed it away carefully to avoid contact with the pristine Italian paintwork of Alasdair's, and, with a cool little wave to him, turned to the child in apology as she drove off. 'Sorry about that.'

After the shock of meeting Alasdair Drummond again, Kate was halfway home before her attention returned to the tense, silent child behind her. 'Are you all right, Abby?'

The little girl looked up at Kate, her eyes desperately worried behind her spectacles. Her lower lip trembled. 'Does it hurt a lot to have a baby, Miss Dysart?'

Kate chose her words carefully. 'I can't speak from personal experience, Abby, but all six of my assorted nephews and nieces arrived without much trouble. Don't worry. I'm sure your mother will be fine,' she added firmly. And sent up a fervent prayer that she was right.

Kate's home was one of a pair of small cottages a

mile past the village itself. Situated deep in rural Herefordshire, Foychurch was a friendly place, with inhabitants who made Kate so welcome to the close-knit community from her first day at the village school that she'd soon felt as much part of it as she did at home in Stavely.

When they arrived Kate unlocked the front door, which opened directly into the sitting room, and ushered her guest inside.

'What a sweet little house, Miss Dysart,' said Abby in admiration.

'Just right for one,' Kate agreed, as she took the child's coat. 'Sit down and make yourself at home, while I make some tea and find something for you to drink.'

The phone rang while Kate was in the tiny, galley-style kitchen.

'Miss Dysart? Jack Spencer. Tim gave me your number. I gather my niece is with you?'

'That's right, Mr Spencer.'

'Look, Miss Dysart, I'm really sorry about this, but I'm stuck here at Heathrow for a while. My parents' plane is delayed.'

'I assure you it's no problem. I'll keep Abby safe until you arrive, whatever time it is.' Kate supplied her address, then joined her little guest.

'That was your uncle, Abby. I'm afraid he won't be here for a while. Your grandparents' plane is delayed.'

Abby perched on the edge of the sofa with her fizzy drink, eyeing Kate in distress. 'I'm sorry to be such a nuisance, Miss Dysart.'

'Of course you're not a nuisance!'

The child smiled gratefully. 'Uncle Jack is Mummy's brother,' she confided. 'He's a builder.'

The word conjured up a vision of low-slung jeans and

suntanned torso which went rather well with the voice on the phone.

'In a little while I'll make something to eat, Abby,' said Kate, 'but first I must ring my mother.'

Upstairs in her bedroom, Kate rang home and explained why she might not be home as early as expected next day. 'If it's late before Abby's collected tonight I fancy a long lie-in tomorrow before the drive.'

'Poor little thing,' said Frances Dysart with sympathy. 'I hope everything goes well with the baby.'

'Amen to that. By the way,' Kate added quickly, 'it wasn't my only surprise of the day, Mother. You'll never believe who was waiting for me outside school. Alasdair Drummond turned up out of the blue to ask me out to dinner.'

'Ah, Adam thought he might.'

'You knew about it? Honestly, Mother,' said Kate indignantly, 'you might have warned me.'

'Alasdair wanted to surprise you.'

'He certainly managed that.'

'So *are* you having dinner with him?'

'No way. Even without my little visitor, I had other plans for my evening.'

'Something nice?'

'Total bliss. Early to bed with a book.'

'Oh, Kate!' Frances laughed ruefully. 'Was Alasdair disappointed?'

'Why should he be?' said Kate tartly. 'He's managed perfectly well without my company for a good few years now.'

'I think you should know,' said her mother carefully, 'that Adam's asked him to the christening.'

'He's done *what*?'

'Darling, Adam thought you'd be pleased.'

Conceding that she'd have been euphoric at one time, Kate managed a chuckle. 'Don't worry, Mother, I won't be too rough on the new daddy. How's the new mummy?'

'Very well. Mainly because her son lets Gabriel sleep now and then. Which is more than his father did for me!'

Kate laughed. 'I trust Adam's shouldering his share of the nappy-changing and so on?'

'He's a natural—took to fatherhood like a duck to water. Drive carefully, darling, and give me a ring when you start out.'

Kate stood grinding her teeth for a moment afterwards, furious with Adam for inviting Alasdair to the christening. Alasdair Drummond had been her first love, it was true. And even after all these years his physical presence still had an impact on her hormones. But her brain strongly objected to his assumption that she'd jump at the chance of an evening with him at the snap of his fingers. Alasdair had always been utterly sure of himself, socially and academically, and in that respect he obviously hadn't changed in the slightest. But *she* had. Her eyes narrowed to a dangerous gleam. He would find that Kate Dysart was very different these days from the worshipful little student of the past.

'Miss Dysart?' called a hesitant voice, and Kate jerked out of her reverie and hurried from the room to find her little guest at the foot of the stairs.

'Sorry to be so long, Abby, I've been chatting to my mother on the phone.'

'Could I go to the loo, please?'

Kate ushered Abby up to the tiny bathroom hurriedly. 'Sorry about that,' she apologised when her guest came downstairs. 'I'll have a very quick bath, then I'll make us some supper.'

'I'll get on with some of the reading you've given us for half-term, then.'

'Good girl. I shan't be long,' Kate ran upstairs and stripped off her serviceable navy sweater and skirt, wishing she could lie in a hot bath for hours instead of a scant five minutes before starting on her hair. Afterwards, in jeans, sneakers and sweatshirt, Kate draped a towel round her shoulders under her wet hair and went down to join Abby, who gazed at her in astonishment.

'You look ever so different with your hair down, Miss Dysart!'

Kate smiled. 'Our secret, OK? Right, then, Abby, I know you're a whiz at reading, but how's your cooking?'

'I help Mummy sometimes.' A smile transformed the sober little face.

'Good girl. Do you like pasta?'

'I love it! Can I grate the cheese?'

Tim Cartwright rang while they were occupied, to report that things were going along satisfactorily enough, but it would be hours before the actual birth. He thanked her fervently, requested a talk with his daughter, and afterwards Abby handed the phone back to Kate with a sigh.

'The baby won't be here for a long time yet,' she said despondently, then brightened. 'But Daddy said Mummy's fine and she's sent me a kiss and told me to thank you for being so kind.'

'How nice of her, especially when she's so busy,' said Kate, eyes twinkling, and gave Abby a wooden spoon to stir the tomato sauce. 'Have a taste—very carefully— and tell me what you think.'

There was no space for any activity other than cooking in Kate's kitchen, which meant that supper was eaten from trays on their knees in the sitting room, to Abby's delight.

'This is yummy,' she said, tasting the pasta. 'Just like Mummy's.'

Kate smiled, accepting this for the supreme accolade it was. 'Thank you, Abby. Eat it all, because I'm afraid there's only fruit or cheese afterwards.'

'I don't mind,' declared Abby, and, with the obvious intention of being a good guest, by way of polite conversation asked if Miss Dysart was going away for the holiday.

Touched, Kate explained that she was going home to Stavely for the week. 'In time for my new little nephew's christening,' she explained. 'My brother's baby. He's six weeks old and I'm his godmother, so I'll be the one holding him when the vicar splashes water on his forehead.'

'Gosh,' said Abby, impressed. 'I expect he'll cry.'

'If so I shall hastily hand him back to his mummy!'

'What's his name?'

'Henry Thomas, after both his grandfathers, but known as Hal, his grandma tells me.'

'Have you seen him yet?'

'No. Which is why my brother arranged the christening for half-term, so I could be there.'

Not that she couldn't have driven home to Friars Wood for a fleeting visit before now. But running home at every possible opportunity was an indulgence Kate had made herself crack down on a long time ago.

After supper Abby helped wash up and clear away, by which time Kate's mane of dark hair was dry, and curling down her back in glossy profusion, much to Abby's admiration. As they worked together Kate encouraged her to talk, drawing her out about her life in London before coming to Foychurch, and learned that Abby missed her schoolfriends there, but loved her new home in the country.

'Miss Dysart,' said Abby after a pause, her voice so forlorn Kate's heart was wrung, 'can I ask you something?'

Kate braced herself. 'Ask away.'

'Do you think Mummy will still love me the same when she's got a new baby?'

'I can assure you that she will, Abby,' said Kate, thinking on her feet. 'I've got three sisters and a brother, and *my* mother loves us all. But in a special way for each of us, because we're all different people.' A bit sentimental, she thought wryly, but it was worth it to see the strain fade from the worried little face.

Deciding a dose of mundane television was the best diversion for a while, Kate tuned in to an innocuous game show, and half an hour passed without more heart-searching because Abby, to her great triumph, gave some correct answers to the questions put to the contestants. Before the show ended there was a knock on the door, and Kate opened it to a man with shaggy fair hair, massive shoulders, and a rugged face with laughter lines raying from eyes which looked down at her in blank astonishment.

'Good evening, Does Miss Dysart live here?'

'I'm Katharine Dysart—' But Kate got no further before a small figure hurtled past her and flung itself into the man's arms.

'Uncle Jack, Uncle Jack—you came!'

Abby's uncle swept her up into a bear hug. 'Of course I came, muggins. Sorry I'm late.' He smiled at Kate over the fair head burrowing against his shoulder. 'Jack Spencer. We spoke on the phone.'

'How do you do? Please come in.'

'Down you go, sweetheart.' Abby's uncle set his burden down, his smile warm for Kate. 'My mother's deeply grateful to you, Miss Dysart. She apologises for not coming on with me, but she was feeling rough after the flight, so I dropped her off with my father at Hope House first. My parents send their thanks.'

'It was no trouble at all,' Kate assured him. 'We've had a very nice evening, haven't we, Abby?'

The little girl nodded fervently. 'I helped make supper, Uncle Jack, and we ate it in here because Miss Dysart doesn't have a table, and we watched television, and Daddy rang, but the baby still hasn't come—'

'Whoa!' said her uncle, laughing. 'You've obviously had a ball, chatterbox. Now, let's get you home to bed.'

While Abby made a trip to the bathroom before the ride home, Kate seized the chance of a private word. 'Mr Spencer, when Abby's father reports next will you tell him she's afraid Mummy won't love her anymore once the new baby comes?'

'Good God!' He stared at her, aghast. 'Don't worry. I'll put Tim in the picture the first minute I can.'

'Thank you.' Kate glanced up with a smile as the little girl came hurtling through the door at the foot of the stairs. 'Steady on, there.'

Abby smiled shyly at Kate. 'Thank you very much for having me, Miss Dysart.'

'It was a pleasure, Abby. See you next week when we get back to school.'

Once Jack Spencer had settled his niece in the Jeep he turned to Kate. 'My thanks again, Miss Dysart. My mother's been in a state all the way down the motorway, anxious about both her girls. Not,' he added, 'that it was necessary with Abby. She obviously had a great time here with you.'

'As much as she could do in the circumstances.' Kate smiled at him. 'I wonder if I could ask a favour?'

'Anything at all.'

'Will you let me know when the baby arrives?'

He grinned. 'Right—though you won't thank me for waking you up in the small hours. I'll ring in the morning. Always supposing the new arrival's made it by that time.'

'Heavens, I hope so,' said Kate with feeling. 'For everyone's sake.'

He eyed her curiously. 'You're very young to be a teacher, Miss Dysart. Is this your first year in the job?'

She chuckled. 'No, indeed. Not by a long way.'

'Then you must be older than you look.' He cast a glance at the small face pressed to a window, watching them. 'Time to go. Goodnight. And thank you again.'

Kate went back in the house in a thoughtful mood. Abby's 'Uncle Jack' might not fit her preconceived idea of him exactly; he was older by far for a start. But he looked capable of carrying hods and laying bricks with the best of them.

The phone rang yet again later, when Kate was getting ready for bed, and she snatched it up eagerly. 'Oh—it's you, Alasdair.'

'Sorry to disappoint you,' he said wryly. 'You were obviously expecting someone else.'

'I was.'

'Has your little visitor gone now?'

'Collected by her uncle an hour ago. I was just on my way to bed.'

'Already?'

'I had a busy day, as we teachers do, followed by an evening trying to entertain a little girl desperately anxious about her mother.' She made no attempt to smother a yawn.

'I'm obviously keeping you, so I'll make it brief. What should I buy young Dysart for a christening present?'

'You don't have to buy anything. I'm sure Adam doesn't expect it.'

'You're to be godmother, he tells me. So what have *you* bought?'

'I've asked Adam to keep his eye out for a claret jug.' Kate waited, sure that Alasdair had quite different reasons for the phone call.

'It struck me afterwards,' he went on, 'that I could have doubled back to see you later this evening when you were free.'

Did it really? 'It wouldn't have been convenient, Alasdair. Besides,' she added frostily, 'I'm told I'll be seeing you on Sunday anyway.'

'Ah. You don't approve.' The deep voice, with it's hint of Edinburgh accent, was timber-dry.

'It's nothing to do with me.'

'But if you don't want me there, Kate—'

'Why on earth shouldn't I? We can have a nice chat about old times,' she said sweetly.

'I'd hoped to do that tonight.' He paused. 'I'm back in the UK for good, by the way. Promotion.'

Kate digested this in silence for a moment, then shrugged, unseen. Whether Alasdair lived in Britain, America, or on the moon, made no difference to her any more.

'Congratulations,' she said eventually. 'Discovered a new wonder drug?'

'Something like that. I'll fill you in when we meet.'

'Alasdair, I should have asked this sooner. Whose funeral was it?'

'My grandmother's.'

'I'm so sorry.'

'Thank you. I'll miss her.' He paused. 'Kate, can we meet tomorrow?'

'No can do. I'm driving home after lunch. Goodnight, Alasdair, I'll see you on Sunday—'

'Don't ring off,' he said, in a tone which put her on her guard. 'If I wait until Sunday I probably won't get you alone. And after seeing you again, Kate I'm more determined than ever to solve the mystery.'

'What mystery?' Though she knew well enough.

'Oh, come *on*—you know what I'm getting at. You were the most brilliant physics student of your year at Cambridge, Katherine Dysart. What in hell happened to make you waste your talents on a village school in the back of beyond?'

CHAPTER TWO

KATE held on to her temper with difficulty. 'Look, Alasdair, we went through this last time we met, and the answer's still the same. I don't consider it a waste. I'm a good teacher, and I get damned good results with my pupils. Nor,' she added fiercely, 'do I look on Foychurch as the back of beyond. It's a friendly, thriving village community. Which suits me down to the ground. I'm a country girl born and bred, remember?'

'I do remember. But that doesn't answer my question, Kate. It was common knowledge that your tutor thought he had another Madame Curie in the making,' Alasdair reminded her.

'Then he was sadly mistaken,' she snapped. 'And now we've cleared that up, I'll say goodnight.'

'Kate, listen—'

'Alasdair, I don't *want* to listen. I'm tired. Goodnight.'

Kate liked to sleep with the curtains drawn back, and, in bed at last, she stared for a long time at the dense blackness of the country night sky, restless and wakeful after Alasdair Drummond's probing.

Her older sisters, Leonie and Jess, had early possessed the self-confidence that matched their looks. So had Adam, their brother. But Kate, younger by several years and far less extrovert, had compensated for lack of confidence with a highly developed work ethos, coupled with a brain that had won her a place at Trinity College, Cambridge, to read Physics.

And there she had met Alasdair Drummond, a veteran

of four years at Edinburgh University, and a year at Harvard, and, by the time she'd met him, engaged in research at Trinity. To her incredulous delight, after running into her on her first day Alasdair had taken Kate under his wing, a process which had boosted both her self-confidence and her appearance so rapidly she'd soon been besieged by so many of her male peers she'd been dumbfounded by all the attention. And hadn't cared a bit for any of it, because she'd fallen hopelessly in love with Alasdair Drummond the moment they'd met.

Kate, too intelligent to deceive herself, had known from the start that the passion was one-sided. Alasdair, five years older in age and a lot more than that in experience, had made it plain he was fond of her, and had taken it on himself to protect her from male predators. But she'd had no illusions about his feelings for her. He had treated her like a kid sister, never as a potential lover. Trying hard to be content with the relationship, she'd cheered him on at rugby matches, felt passionately grateful when he'd taken her with him for a drink afterwards, and preened in secret because it had been taken for granted that they were a couple. But the nearest thing to physical contact with Alasdair had been an occasional—and brotherly—peck on the cheek.

Madly in love for the first time, Kate had eventually grown so frustrated her work had inevitably begun to suffer. Then suddenly, just before Alasdair had been due to leave Cambridge for his first job, she'd locked herself away in her room with only her books for company, pleading pressure of work. She'd refused to socialise with anyone, a mystified Alasdair Drummond included. And, though he'd left to work for an international pharmaceutical company soon afterwards, he'd made a habit of contacting Kate occasionally afterwards to check on her progress.

Then Alasdair's job had taken him to the States, and communication between them had become rare. But, while visiting his grandparents in Gloucester on a trip to the UK, he had made time for a memorable visit to her home just before Kate started in her first teaching post. In response to his bluntly expressed disapproval of her choice of career she'd lost her temper completely, told him that what she did with her life was her own affair, not his, ended by ordering him out of the house, and had heard no more from him since—until his reappearance today outside school.

Alasdair Drummond, the brilliant research chemist Kate had known in the past, had risen with meteoric speed in his career; she knew only too well. And the combination of success and maturity, she thought irritably, was probably a terrific turn-on for most women. But not for her.

Kate's phone woke her on the stroke of seven next morning, and she shot up in bed to grab it, breathless as she answered.

'I obviously woke you up, Miss Dysart,' said Jack Spencer with remorse. 'I'm sorry.'

'It doesn't matter,' she assured him. 'Any news?'

'John Spencer Cartwright arrived a few hours ago, yelling his head off and complete with a full set of everything. My sister's in reasonably good shape, apparently—unlike Tim, who's a gibbering wreck.'

Kate chuckled. 'Thanks for letting me know. How's Abby?'

'On cloud nine because her mother talked to her on the phone the moment she could. Tim passed on your message, so Jules made very sure her special girl knew

Mummy loved her to bits.' Jack Spencer added, 'My sister's deeply grateful to you. On all counts.'

'Only too glad to help.'

'Miss Dysart, Abby tells me you're going home for half-term?'

'That's right.'

'When are you leaving?'

'After lunch. I don't have far to go. I'll be home in time for tea.'

'May I ask where "home" is?'

'Stavely. About twenty miles from Pennington.'

'I know it well. Great part of the world. Enjoy your holiday.'

'I will. Thank you for ringing, Mr Spencer.'

Kate dressed, went downstairs to make breakfast, and afterwards tidied up the cottage. She packed her bags, then went next door to tell Mr Reith, her elderly neighbour, that she would be away for the week, checked that he still had her spare key, then accepted his offer of a cup of coffee and stayed chatting to him for half an hour.

Later, when she was setting time switches to turn her lights on after dark, Kate answered a rap on her front door to find a smiling Jack Spencer, in faded jeans and battered leather flying jacket, holding out an enormous sheaf of early spring flowers.

'Good morning, Miss Dysart. These are by way of thanks.'

'How—how very kind,' said Kate, taken aback. 'Please come in.'

'I'm not holding you up?'

'Not at all. Do sit down. Coffee?'

Jack Spencer shook his head regretfully and perched on the cushioned window seat. 'No, thanks. I'm taking Abby and my parents out to lunch shortly, while Tim gets some sleep. Then we're off to the hospital to meet the heir apparent.'

Kate chuckled. 'I bet Abby can hardly wait.'

'My mother likewise,' he assured her, keen blue eyes trained on her face. 'You look different this morning, Miss Dysart.'

'More like a teacher now my hair's tidy, you mean?'

'I suppose I do. Pity to hide those curls away like that—' He flung up a hand. 'Too personal. Sorry.'

She smiled ruefully. 'I'm way past the age of letting my hair hang down my back.'

'If you say so.' He grinned. 'Last night you looked like a schoolgirl.'

'It's a long time since I was, but thanks just the same, Mr Spencer.'

'Call me Jack.'

Kate shook her head. 'Not appropriate.'

'Because you're Abby's teacher?'

She nodded. 'The Head prides himself on knowing parents by their first names, but, along with the rest of the staff, I stick to Mr and Mrs.'

'But I'm not a parent,' he pointed out. 'Uncles don't count.'

Aware that she was still clutching the vast bouquet, bridal fashion, Kate set it down on a table. 'Please thank Mr and Mrs Cartwright for these, Mr Spencer.'

'Actually, the flowers are from me—Miss Dysart.' His eyes crinkled at the corners as he smiled.

'Then thank *you*,' she said, surprised. 'How kind of you to go out of your way to bring them.'

'I came because I wanted to see you again,' he said simply, and stood up. 'I must be off.'

A rather bemused Kate went to the door to open it. 'Goodbye, Mr Spencer.'

'One day I'll get you to call me Jack,' he promised, and strode down the path to his mud-splattered Cherokee, which now had company. A dark blue Maserati was parked behind it.

Kate stared as she saw Alasdair exchange a brief, unsmiling nod with Jack Spencer, who gave her a wink and a conspiratorial grin before he drove off.

Kate stood in her doorway with arms folded, her face expressionless as she watched Alasdair Drummond open her small wicket gate and stroll up the path towards her. His shoulders were less massive than Jack Spencer's, but he was half a head taller, and, though he wore jeans as vintage as her previous visitor's, it was their only point in common. Alasdair wore polished loafers with a transatlantic air to them, his casual polo shirt was white, and his sweater a shade of almost-pink a less masculine man would have found hard to carry off. The general effect, she thought with amusement, was the acme of elegance compared with her previous visitor.

But this time, without yesterday's shock clouding her vision, Kate was able to look at Alasdair more objectively. His brown hair, once worn close-cropped, was now long enough to curl a little, and his face was leaner than Kate remembered. But the steel-grey eyes were as searching as ever.

'Hello again, Kate,' he said, his smile wary.

'I didn't expect to see you today, Alasdair.' She backed out of reach as he leaned down towards her. 'Don't tell me—you were just passing?'

He straightened, his eyes irritatingly indulgent. 'No. I drove here specifically to see you. I thought we could have lunch somewhere before you take off for Stavely.'

'Sorry. I've had lunch—'

'With the guy I saw leaving just now?'

Leaving him to draw his own conclusion, Kate motioned him inside the cottage, cautioning him to stoop as he went in. 'Since you've driven so far I'll make some coffee.' She glanced at her watch. 'I needn't leave for half an hour or so.'

'Thank you for sparing the time,' said Alasdair wryly, staring at the huge mass of blooms. 'Impressive little tribute. If I'd come bearing flowers would my welcome have been warmer?'

'Have I been rude?' said Kate, unmoved. 'Sorry, Alasdair.'

'I'm very conscious,' he said, the flavour of Edinburgh very distinct in his voice, 'that I've intruded.'

'Of course you haven't,' said Kate lightly. 'I'll just make that coffee.'

'Can I help?'

'No. Just sit down. You make my house look small.'

'It *is* small. Doll-size, like its owner.' He looked her up and down. 'You haven't grown since I saw you last, Kate.'

'Not in inches. But in maturity just a little, I hope.' Pleased with her exit line, she left him alone.

Alasdair shook his head when she came back with sugar and milk on the coffee tray. 'I drink mine black, remember? You should do; you made it often enough for me at one time.'

'I'd forgotten,' said Kate, rather pleased to find this was the truth. At one time she'd tried so hard to forget everything about Alasdair Drummond, and in minor ways, at least, it seemed she'd succeeded.

Like her other visitor, Alasdair took the window seat, his endless legs stretched out in front of him as he looked round at the small room, which was given an illusion of space by an inglenook fireplace and Kate's knack of keeping the curtains drawn back on the walls to expose the entire window.

'Do you light that every day?' he asked, indicating the log fire laid ready.

'No. Only on winter weekends, when I have time to clear it up in the mornings afterwards.' Kate perched on the edge of a chair she normally never used, hoping its bronze velvet looked good with her yellow sweater.

Alasdair drank some of his coffee, regarding her steadily over the rim of his mug. 'The man I saw leaving just now—is he important, Kate?'

'Yes,' she said without hesitation. It wasn't a total lie. Jack Spencer *was* important—to his niece, his mother, his sister, and probably to several more women besides. Maybe a wife, for all she knew. It wouldn't hurt Alasdair to think he was important to Kate Dysart, too. 'How about you, Alasdair? You must have someone important in your life?'

He shook his head. 'Not any more. I shared an apartment with a lady until recently, but that's over now.'

'Why?'

'I suppose you could say she dumped me. Amy liked her New York lifestyle too much to try life in the UK with me.'

Which was enlightening.

'Too bad,' said Kate coolly. 'Where will you be based?'

'Near enough to commute. For the time being, at least.'

'Where from?'

'Gloucester. My grandmother left the house to me.' He finished his coffee and stood up. 'I've held you up long enough.'

Kate went with him to the door. 'Sorry about lunch.'

'Maybe I'll be luckier tomorrow.' He gave her a wry, assessing look. 'In fact, Miss Dysart, I'm likely to get a far warmer welcome from your family than I have from you.' When she showed no sign of penitence Alasdair's jaw tightened. 'The man I saw leaving just now—is he coming on Sunday?'

'No. My family don't know about him yet.' Which was true enough. 'Thanks for coming, Alasdair. See you in church.'

He took her by the shoulders, looking into her eyes. 'Cool reception or not, it's good to see you, Kate.'

She returned the look head-on, doggedly ignoring her body's reaction to his touch. 'It's good to see you, too, Alasdair.'

'I'd prefer a touch more enthusiasm!' He stooped to kiss her cheek, paused for an instant, then kissed her again, his mouth hard and hot on hers. 'See you tomorrow, Kate.'

She shut the door after he'd gone and sat down with a thump, needing time to get herself together. How she'd longed for him to kiss her at one time. And in some ways it had been worth waiting for. Alasdair was as good at kissing as he was at everything else. Kate gave a sudden gurgle of laughter. Normally her only Saturday morning encounters were with the postman and old Mr Reith next door. *This* morning had been in a different league altogether. Jack, as he wanted her to call him, was something new in her experience of men. Not a rough diamond, by any means, but compared with expensively educated Alasdair he was no smooth sophisticate either. Nevertheless, Jack Spencer's in-your-face directness was refreshing. He'd made it flatteringly plain he found her appealing.

Kate felt a surge of triumph as she took her bags out

to the car. From the way Alasdair had kissed her just now, it seemed that these days he found her appealing too. For all the good it would do him.

The windows of Friars Wood, the home of four generations of Dysarts, gleamed in welcome in the pale February sunlight when Kate parked under the chestnut tree at the end of the terrace. The garden was in transition time, waking up from winter to spring, with cushions of snowdrops, clumps of daffodils about to burst into bloom, mauve heather flanked by creamy yellow primroses and purple crocus, and Kate went slowly up the steps, viewing it all with her usual sense of homecoming. Then her eyes lit up as the door to Friars Wood flew open and revealed her tall brother, grinning broadly as he held up the small bundle in his arms.

'You're late, Auntie. Wake up, Son,' Adam instructed his baby. 'Time to meet your godmother.' He swept Kate into a hug with his free arm, and gave her a kiss. 'Hi, half-pint. Want to hold him?'

'Of course I want to hold him!' She dumped down her holdall and held out her arms for her tiny godson. 'Hello, little nephew,' she said softly, smiling down into unfocused blue eyes. 'Oh, thank *goodness*; you take after your mother.'

'He does not,' said Adam indignantly. 'He looks like me.'

Kate eyed his black curly hair and dark eyes in amusement. 'Apart from blue eyes and a wisp of hair as fair as Gabriel's, he's the spitting image,' she mocked, then turned with a smile as her mother came hurrying along the hall from the kitchen.

'Darling,' said Frances, arms outstretched. 'I didn't hear the bell.'

'It didn't ring; I was watching from the window,' said Adam, relieving Kate of his son.

Kate hugged her mother, then grinned as Gabriel Dysart dashed in through the front door. 'Hi, how are you Mumsy?'

'Very pleased with myself,' said Adam's wife, hugging her in turn, and waved a hand at her son. 'Just look at him, Kate. Wasn't I clever?'

'You couldn't have done it without me,' Adam reminded her.

'True,' said Gabriel, laughing, 'But I did the lion's share.'

Kate went into the kitchen with the others, to be given tea and cake and all the latest news of the family. Shortly afterwards her father came in from walking the dog, and Adam fended off the excited retriever while Tom Dysart held his daughter close and demanded all the latest news from Foychurch. Kate sat patting Pan's golden head while she regaled the family with the events of the night before, then sent Adam out to her car to fetch the flowers and explained that her pupil's uncle had given them to her by way of thanks.

'Goodness, how extravagant,' said Frances Dysart when she saw them. 'Enough to make two arrangements for tomorrow, Kate. I've done the church, but I hadn't got round to the house yet. You don't mind if we use them, darling?'

'Of course not. That's why I brought them home.'

'I hear you refused Alasdair's invitation to dinner, by the way,' accused Adam.

Kate wrinkled her nose at him. 'I had other commitments.'

Her brother eyed her warily. 'You know I've invited him to the christening on Sunday?'

'Yes. Though I can't imagine why.'

Adam shrugged. 'When he put some of his grand-mother's furniture into auction at Dysart's he stood me lunch at the Chesterton. I asked him if he'd like to come, and he accepted like a shot. I thought you'd be pleased.'

'He means well,' said Gabriel indulgently, smiling over her son's head.

Kate nodded, resigned. 'I know. And that's quite enough about Alasdair Drummond. Give me the important news. Who else is coming?'

'Leo and Jonah, of course,' said Frances, 'but without the children for once. Jonah's parents are taking them to Paris to Disneyland this weekend.'

'Greater love hath no grandparents,' said Tom piously.

'How about Jess?'

'Not this time,' said Frances, filling teacups. She smiled at Kate. 'She confirmed last night that she's pregnant again.'

'And Lorenzo's keeping her wrapped in cotton wool!' Kate grinned, looked at the downy head cradled close to Gabriel's breast, intercepted the tender look Adam gave his wife and felt a fleeting pang of envy. But dismissed it. The increasing number of her siblings' progeny was quite high enough without adding to it herself.

'How about Fenny?' she asked. 'Is she going to make it?'

'Someone's driving her down this evening, appar-ently,' said Tom, shaking his head. 'She won't take her car to college.'

'Because there's always some clown on hand ready to ferry her wherever she wants to go,' said Adam, grinning.

'More than one,' said Gabriel. 'And she doesn't care a fig for any of them. Just good friends, she says.'

'At her age,' Frances said thankfully, '"just good friends" sounds very comforting to me.'

Soon afterwards Adam and Gabriel took their son off to the Stables for his bath and supper, promising to return with him later for dinner.

'Though whether Fenny will be home in time to share it is uncertain,' said Frances, chuckling. 'But she'll ring at some stage. Fen tries not to worry me too much.'

'Your ewe lamb,' teased Tom.

'Come over with us, Kate,' said Adam. 'I'll show you the jug I found for you.'

She looked at her mother. 'Unless there's anything I can do to help?'

'No, darling. It's a very simple meal tonight.'

Adam took charge of the buggy as the three of them walked briskly to hurry the baby into the warmth of the stable block which had been Adam's private quarters since his eighteenth birthday.

'I'll look on while you do the hard part,' Kate told Gabriel. 'Or is Daddy going to do bathtime?'

'We share the process unless I'm late home,' said Adam as they went upstairs. 'Actually, I wanted a word on the quiet, Kate,' he added, cuddling his son while Gabriel filled the baby bath. 'I take it you weren't too pleased to see Alasdair?'

'Not at first.' She wagged a finger at him. 'Nor with you, either. You might have warned me! After all this time it was a bit of a shock to find him waiting for me outside school, of all places.'

'He wanted to surprise you.'

'I've never met this Alasdair, of course,' said Gabriel,

undressing her squirming baby, 'but I gather he's done well for himself.'

'Unlike me, he's done what everyone expected of him. And now he's here to run the UK operation of the pharmaceutical giant who head-hunted him from Cambridge,' said Kate. 'Gosh, the baby does wriggle, doesn't he?'

'Terrified me the first time,' agreed Adam, and hooked his hands under his kicking son's armpits while Gabriel did the sponging—a process Hal objected to at the top of his voice.

'Pass him over quickly,' begged Gabriel, and hastily wrapped her son in a warm towel to cuddle him. 'Dash down and get his bottle, darling, please.'

'You're not feeding him yourself, then?' said Kate, mopping up splashes.

'No. Not that I'm sorry. This way we can share the night-time feeds. At least that's the theory,' added Gabriel, chuckling. 'But I wake up anyway.'

'I bet Adam doesn't when it's your turn!' Kate watched while her nephew was fastened into a stretchy sleepsuit. 'Do you enjoy motherhood, Gabriel?'

Her sister-in-law turned with a smile, cradling her restless son against her shoulder. 'Just between you and me, Kate, I hadn't thought to go in for it quite yet, but now he's here I wouldn't give him back.'

'Neither would I,' said Adam, as he joined them. 'We never get enough sleep any more, but this, we're assured, will improve with time.' He kissed his wife as he handed over the bottle of formula. 'We'll leave you to it, sweetheart.'

When Adam unwrapped the silver-mounted crystal jug he'd found on his travels Kate stroked it with pleasure.

'Perfect. But how much would you have got at auction for a beauty like this?'

'Irrelevant. You can have it for the money I gave for it,' he assured her. 'But look, if you can't afford it—'

'I most definitely can. I've been saving up ever since Gabriel told me she was pregnant.' Kate smiled. 'I rather took it for granted you'd ask me to be godmother.'

'You knew I would,' he said gruffly, and gave her a searching look. 'Now we're on our own, is everything all right with you, Kate?'

'Always the same old question,' she said, resigned. 'And it's always the same old answer, Adam. Contrary to *some* people's belief, I like my life and I love my job.'

'"Some people" meaning Alasdair?'

'Who else? Due to my famed qualifications he thinks I'm mad to teach at a village school.' Kate shot him a look. 'Do you still agree with him?'

'Of course not. Like everyone else, I was a bit surprised at first, but it's very obviously what you want to do, so I'm happy for you.'

'You don't mind that I'm never likely to win the Nobel prize, then?'

'No way.' Adam smiled crookedly. 'In fact, I'd rather you met some guy who'll make you as happy as I am with Gabriel.'

'Don't hold your breath,' Kate warned him, laughing. 'If I do feel the need for a male presence in my life one day I'll get a dog like Pan.'

Adam chuckled. 'Tell me when and I'll buy you one.' He eyed her curiously. 'Now he's back in this country, will you be seeing Alasdair more often?'

Kate shook her head. 'I doubt it. I live in deepest Herefordshire, and Alasdair intends living in the

Gloucester house his grandmother left him. It's not exactly next door.'

'Near enough for him to come calling round twice in two days,' he reminded her.

Kate's mouth compressed. 'I'll make sure he doesn't make a habit of it.'

'Is there someone else, then?'

She shrugged impatiently. 'You know perfectly well I see Toby Anderson and Phil Dent when I'm home.'

Adam rolled his eyes. 'The accountant and the sports master. Wild passionate affairs both, of course.'

'How do you know what they're like?' said Kate indignantly.

'Because you go out with both of them. I can't see you leaping in and out of bed with two blokes, turn and turn about!'

Kate gave him a shove, laughing. 'Not everyone wants wild, passionate affairs.'

'How about marriage, then?'

'One day, maybe,' she said lightly. 'At the moment I'm happy with my role of maiden aunt to the Dysart young.'

CHAPTER THREE

NEXT morning, Fenny knocked on Kate's door and came in with two mugs of tea, then perched, yawning, on the end of the bed.

'This is very good of you,' said Kate, surprised. 'Thanks, Fen.'

'My pleasure. So how are things, schoolteacher?' Fenny's green eyes sparkled below a tangled mass of hair as dark as Kate's. 'Life in the sticks as scintillating as usual?'

'A laugh a minute,' agreed Kate, and sat up to drink her tea. 'Who drove you home last night?'

'Prue's boyfriend. She came home for the weekend, too.'

'But she lives in Marlborough.'

'After he dropped her off he insisted on driving me all the way here, so who was I to refuse?'

'You should have invited him in to supper.'

'No way.' Fenny grinned. 'Time for that when it's *my* boyfriend, not someone else's.'

'You're incorrigible!'

'But cute with it.'

'Oh, yes,' sighed Kate. 'You're cute, all right. But don't push your luck, Fen.'

'With blokes, you mean? Don't worry. I'm quite sensible really. *And* I'm going to wear a skirt today.'

'No! I suppose that means I have to as well, then.'

'I bet you were anyway, Miss Sobersides.'

Kate gave her a sharp look. 'Is that how you see me?'

'Lately, yes,' said Fenny candidly. 'So for heaven's sake let that gorgeous hair down today, Kate—literally, I mean—and wear something to knock the vicar's eye out.'

'Is that why you brought me the tea? So you could give me a pep talk about my looks?'

'I brought the tea,' said Fenny indignantly, 'out of the goodness of my heart!'

Kate laughed. 'Then thank you kindly.'

'I wonder if Adam and Gabriel got any sleep last night? That baby has a powerful pair of lungs.' Fenny slid off the bed and stretched. 'I shall be back shortly with your breakfast.'

'You will not! I'm getting up—'

'Mother said you're to stay where you are for a bit. Best place to be; it's freezing outside. I hope you brought your thermals.' Fenny paused in the doorway. 'By the way, Gabriel and the grandmas are wearing hats—Leo, too.'

Kate groaned. 'No one told me.'

'Mother was discussing it downstairs with Dad just now. I think she has something in mind for you.'

'Don't tell me she's *bought* me a hat?'

Fenny giggled. 'If so you'll just have to grin and wear it!'

But Frances Dysart, it transpired, had not gone shopping for a hat. She arrived a little later with a breakfast tray, and Fenny, eyes dancing, following behind with a large hat box.

'The godmother really should wear a hat, Kate,' said Frances the traditionalist, and laid the tray across her daughter's knees. 'I know you don't have one, so I had a search on top of the cupboards in our dressing room. Open the box, Fenny.'

Rolling her eyes at Kate behind her mother's back, Fenny removed several layers of silver paper from a striking hat in pale, dark-spotted fur.

'Wow,' said Kate faintly. 'Please tell me that's *fake* ocelot, Mother!'

'Of course it is. Though the polite word is *faux,* darling.'

Kate eyed it doubtfully. 'Do you really think it's me?'

'You'll look great in it,' said Fenny unexpectedly. 'Lots of make-up on your eyes and the hat worn dead straight above them—very sexy!'

'I'm not sure that was *my* intention,' said Frances dryly. 'But she's right, Kate. You'll look perfect. Now, eat your breakfast.'

'I can't remember you in anything like that, Mother.'

'It was Grandma Dysart's, bought for a winter wedding. She had a coat with matching cuffs—there's a photograph somewhere.' Frances shooed Fenny to the door. 'Right, then, Kate, we'll see you later.'

Kate ate her breakfast thoughtfully, her eyes on the hat on the dressing table. At last she could resist it no longer, and got out of bed, brushed her hair back behind her ears and pulled on the hat. Relieved to sniff lavender instead of camphor, she stood back, eyeing the result. Even with striped pyjamas, and without layers of eye make-up, the fur hat was dramatic. And surprisingly flattering.

When Kate got downstairs she found Mrs Briggs, her mother's cleaner, dealing with potatoes in the kitchen sink while Frances carved slices from a ham. Kate greeted Mrs Briggs affectionately, put her breakfast things in the dishwasher, then demanded a job.

'You can slice the turkey, if you like,' said her mother.

'Won't Dad mind? Carving's his specialty.'

'He's gone for a drive. Hal was so wakeful last night I ordered Gabriel and Adam back to bed for a nap. The baby was a bit noisy after they left him here, so Tom and Fenny went out in the car with him to let me get on.' Frances chuckled. 'No matter how cross he is Hal goes to sleep the moment the engine starts.'

Kate listened to the latest news of Stavely from Mrs Briggs as the three of them put the finishing touches to the feast, then went into the dining room to lay out silverware on the vast damask cloth that only came out for special occasions. Afterwards Kate sent her mother up to dress, checked on the arrangements she'd made the day before with Jack Spencer's flowers, then returned to the kitchen when she heard Fenny come in with her father and Adam.

'I hope your hourly rate isn't too exorbitant, Fen,' said Adam, relieving her of his sleeping son.

'You may ply me with champagne later,' she assured him.

'Mother says you're to go up and change, Dad,' warned Kate.

'Shouldn't I be doing the carving?'

'All taken care of while you were touring the countryside,' she assured him.

'Thanks, Dad,' said Adam gratefully. 'Gabriel and I slept like logs for a couple of hours.'

'Which was the object of the exercise,' said his father, on his way to the door. 'Go on, get your lad dressed in his best bib and tucker. People will be arriving soon.'

'Don't forget, Kate, leave your hair down,' ordered Fenny as they went upstairs, then bit her lip. 'Sorry! I'm bossy, but I mean well.'

'I know. I tried the hat on, by the way. It looks rather good.'

'Which, translated from Kate-speak, means it's a knockout!'

Later, in a clinging amber knit dress bought with her Christmas present money, Kate eyed herself critically in the mirror. Her hair, brushed back to reveal her ears, left the emphasis on the eyes she thought of as her best feature. The dark-rimmed irises were translucent hazel shot with gold, and made up today with a drama she normally never bothered with. And probably wouldn't have bothered with now, she admitted sheepishly, if Alasdair Drummond hadn't been invited. The sound of cars drawing up outside sent her to the window to see her sister Leonie and her husband, Jonah Savage, greeting Gabriel's parents, and Kate yanked on tall-heeled brown suede boots and hurried from the room to bang on Fenny's door.

'Get a move on. Leo's arrived.'

After a flurry of hugs and kisses everyone was soon crowded into the kitchen as usual, catching up with each others news as they drank coffee. Gabriel handed her son over to her mother, so that Laura Brett could indulge in extravagant baby-worship as she told her grandson how beautiful he was, and, after contributing her own share, Leo drew Kate aside.

'You look good, love. Great to see that hair down for once. All set to carry out your duties?'

Kate flicked a hand at Leonie's violet wool suit. 'You look pretty gorgeous yourself, Mrs Savage. But I'm a tad nervous about the godmother bit. I just hope I don't drop my nephew in the font.'

Jonah Savage hugged Kate and Fenny in turn. 'Hi

there, you gorgeous creatures. Invited anyone along to-day?'

'If you mean anyone male, no,' said Kate. 'Fenny wouldn't know which one to choose, for a start.'

'I'm not the only one,' said Fenny, and batted her eyelashes at Jonah. 'Adam says Kate has *two* admirers. Two that he knows about, anyway.'

Kate shot her a startled look, then choked back a laugh. Fenny meant the accountant and the teacher, not the pharmaceutical star and the builder.

'She's got an older flame than that coming today,' said Adam, joining them. 'Remember Alasdair Drummond? He's back from the States, so I asked him along.'

Leonie gave her sister a sharp look. 'You two still in touch, then?'

Kate shrugged. 'Not really. I hadn't heard from him for ages until a couple of days ago.'

'Is he the one you were up at Cambridge with?' asked Fenny.

'For a while. He was a lofty research fellow and I was a humble first-year when we met.'

'Then how on earth did you manage to get friendly?' Fenny pulled a face. 'It wouldn't happen at my Alma Mater.'

Kate shrugged. 'He just happened to be on hand the day I arrived, helped carry my gear, and sort of looked out for me from then on.'

'Her minder. He kept the wolves from her door,' said Adam with satisfaction.

Kate made a face at him and went off to talk to Gabriel's parents, leaving Leonie to gaze after her with troubled eyes.

'I hope that's not starting up again,' she murmured.

'What?' said Fenny curiously.

Leonie sighed. 'Kate had a huge crush on Alasdair Drummond in those days.'

'Reciprocated?'

'No. Which worries me.'

'Kate doesn't look worried.' Jonah comforted his wife. 'Besides, that was years ago. She'll have got over it by this time.'

Fenny's eyes gleamed. 'Or is she still carrying a torch for this Alasdair?'

'I hope not.' Leonie fixed her brother with an accusing eye. 'What gave you the bright idea of asking him here today?'

'I've been doing some business with him. Besides, I like him.' Adam shrugged ruefully. 'And I thought, in my infinite wisdom, that Kate would be pleased. But Gabriel says I'm wrong.'

Leonie sighed. 'Oh, well, it's only for an hour or two. Kate can hardly come to harm with us around.'

'How can she come to any harm?' said Fenny, mystified. 'It's a christening, not an orgy!'

'"Out of the mouth of very babes…"' teased Jonah. 'Your mother's signalling, Leo. Time to put on your hat.'

Fenny pulled a face. 'I'll be the only one with naked hair.'

'Good thing St Paul can't be here, then,' said Jonah. 'Women's hair was his weakness. Mine too.' He leered at his wife. 'One of them, anyway.'

'Don't be rude,' said Fenny, sticking her tongue out at him. 'If Kate heard you she'd start scraping her hair back in a bun again, so keep your weaknesses to yourself, Jonah Savage.'

A few minutes later the newest addition to the family was swathed in the shawl that served all Dysart christenings, and his various female relatives were ready and hatted when Fenny dashed to join them, wearing a man's navy coat and clumpy, platform-soled shoes, her hand held up for attention.

'For pity's sake tell her she looks great,' she hissed, then stood aside nonchalantly when Kate appeared in her long, fitted coat of bronze wool, hair rippling in a shining dark cascade down her back, the fake-fur hat set straight over eyes that looked around in question.

'What do you think? Will I do?'

'You look amazing, Kate!' said Gabriel, handing her son to Adam. 'Straight out of *Doctor Zhivago*.'

'The hat looks wonderful on you, darling,' said Tom Dysart, and exchanged a smile with his wife. 'I remember my mother in it.'

'You put us all in the shade,' Leonie assured her sister warmly.

Adam grinned at Kate over his son's head. 'Prepare yourself for a photo call after the ceremony, godmother.'

'When are the godfathers arriving?' she asked, as everyone made a move.

'Hopefully they're at the church right now, along with everyone else.' Adam looked at his watch. 'At least Jeremy Blyth will be. But punctuality was never one of Charlie's strong suits.'

'I thought you had a row with Charlie Hawkins,' said Leonie, as they went out to the cars.

'All in the past,' Adam told her, smiling at Gabriel.

'Life's too short to be at odds with old friends,' agreed his wife. 'The other godfather is *my* old friend.'

'The famous Jeremy Blyth, art dealer extraordinaire,' said Harry Brett, grinning at his daughter. 'What's he giving Hal for a present, Gabriel? A Picasso?'

'We should be so lucky!'

When the family party arrived at the church a small crowd of people were gathered outside in the icy sunshine. Towering above the rest, Alasdair Drummond, superbly dark-suited, was deep in conversation with a similarly formal Charles Hawkins, who had been friends with Adam Dysart since their first day at school. But Jeremy Blyth, a slender man with sleek fair hair, was exquisite and unmistakable in a pearl-grey suit, with bow tie and waistcoat in lilac silk.

Kate saw Alasdair stop mid-sentence as he caught sight of her, and gave him a brilliant smile as Gabriel hurried to kiss Jeremy Blyth and Charlie before moving on to smile at the man next in line.

'By a process of elimination,' said Gabriel, 'you must be Alasdair Drummond. I'm Gabriel Dysart.'

'Then Adam's a lucky man,' he assured her. 'It was good of him to invite me here today.'

'Hospitable bloke,' said Charlie, clapping Adam on the shoulder. 'May I say you look stunning, Mrs Dysart?'

'As many times as you like,' Gabriel assured him. 'Come and meet your godson.'

After a round of greetings and kisses with friends and neighbours, everyone moved inside for the service. Kate received Henry Thomas Dysart into her arms, and looked up to meet grey eyes regarding her from the background with a heat which brought her lashes down to hide the triumph in her own. Alasdair Drummond might have thought of her in a brotherly way in the past, but that, Kate knew without doubt, was no longer the case. Ignoring a rush of excitement totally unsuitable to her surroundings, she kept her attention firmly on the stirring bundle in her arms and, in unison with Jeremy

Blyth and Charlie Hawkins, made the necessary affirmations about her part in young Hal's future welfare.

The baby objected so volubly to the holy water there was a ripple of delighted laugher, and Kate, not without trepidation, took him into her arms again and rocked him against her shoulder. Gabriel handed over a pacifier, Kate slid it into the protesting mouth, and instantly there was peace to finish the service and for the photographs outside before the short drive back to Friars Wood.

Mrs Briggs, with the help of her daughter, had been busy in their absence. When the guests were shown straight into the large, south-facing dining room the table looked magnificent, with the flowers Kate had arranged as centrepiece, and an array of food, hot and cold, flanked by glasses which glittered in the rays from the setting sun, waiting for the champagne Charlie Hawkins, successful wine merchant, had provided as part of his gift to his godson.

Master Dysart was changed into something more comfortable, then provided with milk administered by Laura Brett, who persuaded Frances Dysart to keep her company on a sofa while the daughters of the house served guests with the celebration meal.

It was some time before Kate, now minus the hat, had time to talk to Alasdair, but at last she felt obliged to join him on his perch on the ledge in the big square bay window.

'Have you been introduced to everyone?' she asked.

'Adam saw to that.' He gave her a look which brought heat to her face. 'You looked breathtaking in that hat, Kate—straight from a Russian fairy tale.'

'Why, thank you, kind sir,' she said lightly.

'You should always wear that glorious hair down.'

'Don't you start! It was OK when I was eighteen, but I'm a big girl now, Alasdair.'

His soft laughter raised hairs on her spine.

'Not really, Kate. More a pocket Venus!'

'What are you saying to make this delightful creature blush?' asked Jeremy Blyth, joining them.

'Do sit down,' said Kate, patting the broad ledge beside her. 'Alasdair was just paying me a compliment. I think.'

'As well he might, my dear.' Jeremy shook his head. 'I wonder if my darling Gabriel had any idea what she had to compete with when she met Adam? You Dysarts are a handsome lot.'

'Including the baby of the family,' agreed Alasdair, looking across the room to Fenny, who was chattering to Harry Brett and Jonah. 'That charmer was a gawky little kid when I saw her last.'

'But little girls get bigger every day, dear boy,' said Jeremy, and turned to Kate. 'Now then, fellow godparent, at what point should we converge, like the Magi, to present our gifts to the infant?'

'After the cake is cut and everyone is refilled with champagne for the toasts,' she said promptly.

'Talking of which,' said Alasdair, getting up, 'your glass is empty, Kate. Let me get you a refill.'

'Just lemonade, please.'

'Oh, come on, Kate, you must have champagne in honour of your godson,' he protested.

'Not for me, thanks,' she said with finality.

'Is your aversion to alcohol in general, my dear?' asked Jeremy gently after Alasdair left them.

'Not at all. Just champagne—or any kind of wine, really.' Kate smiled at him, then beckoned to Charlie Hawkins. 'We hand over the presents after the cake is cut, Charlie. Not that mine will be a surprise. Adam found it for me.'

'Do tell,' said Jeremy promptly.

'Crystal claret jug—silver-mounted, but empty.' Kate grinned at Charlie. 'I'll come to you for the claret when Hal's eighteen.'

'I'll keep you to that, my lovely,' he promised, and thrust a hand through his red hair. 'I was over the moon when Adam asked me to be godfather, I can tell you. Never expected it in the circumstances.'

'A more tactful person wouldn't ask, but I'm famed for my lack of finesse,' said Jeremy, eyes gleaming. 'What circumstances, dear boy?'

'Adam and I fell out over a woman a while back— before he met Gabriel,' confessed Charlie. 'Stupid mistake on my part. All over now, thankfully. Gabriel persuaded him to let bygones be bygones.'

'Adam didn't take much persuading—he was only too glad to mend the rift,' said Kate, and looked up with a smile as Alasdair returned with her glass. 'Thank you.'

'Unadulterated, I swear,' he promised her.

'Good,' Kate got up in response to Leonie's beckoning hand. 'If you'll excuse me, gentlemen, duty calls.'

'Gabriel and Adam are about to cut the cake while Dad and Jonah top up the champagne glasses,' said Leonie when Kate joined her. She gave her sister a keen look. 'So. How are things with Alasdair?'

Kate thought it over. 'Friendly, I suppose.'

'On your part maybe!' Leonie's dark eyes lit with a triumphant gleam. 'But unless I'm mistaken—which I never am—now you've met up again Alasdair feels a whole lot more than friendly towards *you*, little sister.'

CHAPTER FOUR

ADAM made a speech, toasts were drunk to Henry Thomas Dysart, and once the champagne had gone round again, accompanied by slices of the frosted christening cake made by Laura Brett, the baby was put down to kick on a blanket and receive his tributes.

Kate smiled as everyone gathered round to look on. 'Adam found the jug for me, so it's no surprise, but at least I know I've got the genuine article.'

Her father patted her shoulder. 'Good choice, darling.'

Charlie Hawkins sighed regretfully. 'I did *not* buy these through Dysart's; it seemed too much of a cheek. But I wish I had now, in case they're not up to scratch.'

Adam assured his friend that the set of antique silver wine labels was of impeccable quality. 'But I bet you paid over the odds for them.'

'No matter,' said Charlie with dignity, and gave way to Jeremy Blyth, who kissed Gabriel's hand as he presented her with a large box.

'Such a trial, dear heart,' he said, 'buying a present for a Dysart child. I toyed with the idea of a modest little painting, but in the face of his parents' combined expertise I hadn't the courage. So I played safe.' He touched a manicured finger to the sleeping baby's face. 'Have fun with it, Henry Thomas Dysart. And may you grow up to be as handsome as your mother.'

Gabriel's eyes widened as she took a battered teddy bear from the box. Some of the guests looked taken aback, but Adam shot Jeremy a respectful look as he felt for the button embedded in the bear's ear.

'A Steiff, no less, and a pretty old one, too.'

'But not frightfully valuable,' Jeremy assured him. 'I lusted after one of the limited-edition black bears manufactured when the *Titanic* went down, but the funds wouldn't stretch. And if they had you couldn't have allowed him to play with it.'

'He'll certainly play with this one,' Gabriel assured him, and kissed Jeremy's cheek with affection. 'Thank you.'

Alasdair waited until the other guests had handed over their gifts before presenting his, and received an appreciative smile from Adam when Gabriel unwrapped a shallow silver drinking bowl with double handles.

'A Scottish *quaich*! Very appropriate. Many thanks, Alasdair.'

At last, when guests were beginning to leave, the moment arrived that Kate had known all along was unavoidable.

'I want a word in private before I go,' said Alasdair, drawing her aside.

It was the last thing Kate wanted, with several interested pairs of eyes turned in their direction, and she made no attempt to hide her reluctance as she led the way to the study. 'Only for a moment, then. I should be seeing people off.'

'I'm not leaving until you promise to see me again,' he announced, and stood with his shoulders against the closed door.

'How very masterful. Are you barring my way until I agree?' she said lightly.

'Yes,' he returned, not lightly at all.

'Oh, very well. What did you have in mind?'

'Just dinner, and a talk over old times.'

'This week?'

'No, next year,' he said irritably. 'Are you always so hard to pin down, Kate Dysart?'

She shrugged, resigned. 'All right, Alasdair. Thursday, then. If that suits you.'

His jaw tightened. 'I'll make it suit me. Otherwise you'd probably refuse altogether. I'll come for you at seven. Where shall we go?'

'Somewhere local, please. I'll consult Adam.'

Alasdair moved away from the door. 'I'll ring you to see if I need to book. And to make sure you don't change your mind.' He shook his head ruefully. 'You were a lot easier to deal with in the old days, Katharine Dysart.'

'You whistled and I danced,' she agreed, and went to the door he held open for her. She gave him a cool little smile as she brushed past. 'But I've grown up a bit since then.'

Kate was in bed that night before she had any peace to reflect on Alasdair's part in the day. Once the Bretts had gone, and Leonie and Jonah had been waved off shortly afterwards, the rest of the family had talked over the day with satisfaction as they ate a supper of leftovers. But it had been left to Fenny to demand why Alasdair had talked with Kate in private.

'Fenny!' said Frances in disapproval.

'She only asked what we're all panting to know,' said Adam, and eyed Kate expectantly. 'Are you seeing him again?'

She made a face at him. 'Yes. I couldn't get out of it a second time.'

'Why should you want to get out of it?' he asked, surprised.

'Perhaps,' said Gabriel perceptiently, 'Alasdair was taking things too much for granted?'

'Something like that,' Kate agreed. 'I just wish he hadn't chosen to turn up at school. Imagine the ribbing I'll get from the rest of the staff next week!'

'He can turn up outside my college any time he likes,' said Fenny with envy. 'You don't need someone as tall as Alasdair, anyway, Kate. He'd suit a beanpole like me much better.'

'I seriously doubt that,' jeered Adam. 'He prefers women with brains.'

'Hey!' objected Fenny indignantly, then threw up a hand. 'OK, OK, I may not be as clever as Kate, but I do have *some* brains.'

Kate had changed the subject hastily by asking about the best place for a meal these days, and shortly afterwards Gabriel and Adam had taken their son home, and Kate had been able to go to bed, in urgent need of time to herself.

Alasdair's reappearance in her life, she reflected, was nowhere near as welcome as he obviously assumed it was. After their final meeting, when he'd been so angry with her for what he'd called wasting her talents, her resentment had been so fierce she'd done her best to forget she'd ever met him. But, she admitted honestly, Alasdair still held the old physical appeal for her, whether she liked it or not. She'd been a late developer where the opposite sex was concerned, and Alasdair had been the first to arouse any sexual feelings in her. Now he'd matured into a powerfully attractive man he still had the same ability to make her pulse race, but she didn't need her famous qualifications to recognise it as pure basic chemistry. An inconvenience, but nothing more than that. Alasdair Drummond would be given no chance to disrupt her life a second time.

Because Fenny, as usual, preferred not to drive herself to college, instead of letting her go by train Kate gave her a lift back next day, stayed for a while to drink coffee and chat with some of Fenny's friends in her room in hall, then drove back to Stavely in time for dinner alone with her parents for the first time.

'So what do you want to do with the rest of your week?' asked Frances.

'As little as possible. I'm going out with Toby tomorrow night, but otherwise I thought I'd just catch up on some sleep, walk the dog, and wheel the baby out in his buggy now and then. But first I quite fancy a trip into Pennington. Are you free to go out to play tomorrow, Mother? I need some clothes.'

'When is your mother not free to go shopping for clothes?' said Tom, laughing.

'Very true,' agreed his wife with relish. 'I'd love to, Kate. I've got a dentist's appointment there after lunch, but otherwise I'm yours. What did you have in mind?'

'Nothing exciting. A new bathing suit for swimming with the school, some underwear—and lots of window shopping.' Kate smiled. 'Village post office apart, Foychurch is a bit lacking that way. I yearn to gaze into shop windows full of things I can't afford.'

When Alasdair rang, halfway through the meal, Kate excused herself and left the room to speak to him.

'Have you sorted out somewhere for Thursday, Kate?'

'I'm told the Forrester's Arms is the local in-place for food these days. Only five miles away and no need to book. See you about seven, then, Alasdair—'

'Hold on, what's the rush?'

'I'm in the middle of dinner,' said Kate firmly. 'See you Thursday.' And she returned to the meal, wondering why Alasdair Drummond, who hadn't been in contact for years, now seemed unable to let a day go by without getting in touch.

Thoroughly enjoying the shopping expedition next day, Kate bought a plain navy swimsuit from a sports shop, some cotton underwear from a chainstore and re-sisted all her mother's coaxing on the subject of a new dress for her evening with Alasdair. 'The one I wore for the christening was a pricey little number, so I might as well get some mileage out of it.'

And nothing Frances could say would change her mind, though Kate's resistance weakened when her mother spotted a pair of cropped trousers in bright coral linen in a window. 'Perfect for the summer—you need something frivolous, so let me treat you,' said her mother firmly. 'I only wish I was young enough to wear them myself.'

Kate gave in without a struggle. And when her mother bought her more underwear, frivolous and lacy this time, Kate's resistance was at an all-time low.

'Come on, you subversive creature,' she said to Frances. 'Let's get out of here before you undermine every principle I've got.'

But Frances went on to buy miniature T-shirts and dungarees for the baby, a lipstick each for Kate and Gabriel, and a bag full of goodies from the food hall before they moved on to as much window gazing as Kate's heart desired. And later, during lunch, Frances was so obviously enjoying the time spent with her daughter Kate felt guilty because she wasn't home to do this kind of thing more often.

Later Frances went off to her dentist, leaving Kate to

haul their shopping back to Dysart's. On her way to the auction house she tripped and dropped one of her parcels, and to her surprise found that the smiling man who retrieved it was Jack Spencer.

'Why, hello there!' Kate returned the smile with pleasure. 'Thank you. As you can see, I've been indulging in some serious retail therapy. How's the new arrival, Mr Spencer?'

'In an incubator for a day or two, but only as a precaution. He's a great little chap.'

'And how about Abby?'

'Happy as a lark now.' He smiled down at her. 'A lot of which is down to you, Miss Dysart.'

'More down to having a new baby brother!'

'How about celebrating his arrival by having lunch with me?'

Kate shook her head regretfully. 'I lunched early with my mother. She's gone off to the dentist.'

'When are you due to meet her again?'

'In an hour or so.'

He eyed her burden with disapproval. 'You're not going to haul those bags round town until then?'

'I was just taking them back to my father at the auction house.'

'Ah!' He nodded in comprehension. 'You're one of those Dysarts.'

'The family business. I was going to beg a coffee while I wait.'

'Have one with me at the Chesterton instead.' Without waiting for her consent, he took charge of her bags and hurried her off to the car parked illegally at the kerb. 'They'll give me a sandwich to eat with it while you tell me everything you've been doing since I saw you last.'

With a bemused feeling she was beginning to associate with Jack Spencer, Kate meekly let him hand her up into the black Cherokee Jeep, and raised a quizzical eyebrow as he stowed her parcels in the back.

'A problem?' he asked, as he drove off.

'No. I was just wondering if everyone always does exactly what you want all the time.'

'Pretty much,' he admitted cheerfully.

Kate took a look at his suit, which on close quarters proved to be of quality as good as anything worn by her father or Adam. Or Alasdair. 'Day off today?' she asked.

He shook his fair head, which looked marginally tidier than the last time they'd met. 'Interview.' Again the sidelong grin. 'Though a meeting with you is an unexpected bonus. I was driving past when I spotted you juggling with those bags.'

'You mean you just stopped the car when you saw me?'

'I came to a screaming halt and raced after you like the guy in the TV ad. Only I didn't have any flowers to give you.'

'You've already done that bit!'

He laughed as he turned in to the Chesterton car park. 'So I have.' He glanced at his watch. 'Hurry up. Ten minutes of your hour gone already, so we'll have coffee in the bar.'

Kate's hair was braided into a corn dolly plait, instead of the knot her companion had objected to previously, and she wore jeans and ankle boots and a Barbour jacket over a heavy pink sweater, but as she went through the portals of the elegant hotel she wished she'd chosen something smarter for her shopping spree.

'I'm not really dressed for a place like this,' she muttered, as Jack ushered her into a bar crowded with businessmen talking shop before lunch.

He gave her a morale-boosting look as he seated her at a corner table. 'You look good to me,' he informed her, which had such a ring of truth to it Kate relaxed, and watched Jack Spencer with frank curiosity when he went off to the bar to joke with the man behind it as he placed their order. Neither as tall as Alasdair, nor as lean as her brother, there was nevertheless an air of authority about Jack Spencer that made Kate wonder exactly what kind of building work he was involved in. And at his age what job was he interviewing for? She raised her eyebrows, impressed, when he returned to the table accompanied by a waiter with a tray of coffee and sandwiches.

'That was quick' she said, when the waiter had departed, generously tipped.

'I said you were in a hurry. He must have thought these were for you,' he added wryly, looking at the dainty, crustless selection.

'Eat them two at a time,' she advised.

He laughed, and asked what kind of shopping she'd been doing.

'Clothes to wear for the job. Other than that just window shopping with my mother. I miss that in Foychurch.'

'It can't be the only thing you miss.' Jack Spencer eyed her curiously. 'What do you do for entertainment in a quiet place like that?'

'I keep very busy,' she assured him. 'Teaching is no nine-to-five job. And apart from the usual routine I run the after-school science club, help out on school trips and various fund-raising events, co-produce the school plays. Socially I see a film or share a meal in Hereford with colleagues, and so on. In summer I like grubbing about in my cottage garden, and in winter I belong to the village dramatic society—'

'How about men?' he asked abruptly. 'The one I saw the other day, for starters?'

Kate shrugged. 'Alasdair's an old college friend. He's just returned from the States to work in this country.'

He shot her a searching blue glance. 'Does that mean he'll be monopolising your social life from now on?'

Deciding it was a waste of time to object to this man's bluntness, Kate shook her head. 'I don't let any one person monopolise my social life, Mr Spencer—'

'Jack.' He smiled at her. 'Go on. It's very easy to say. Try it.'

She smiled back. 'Jack, then.'

'Much better,' he said with satisfaction, and held out his cup for a refill. 'Besides this Alasdair, are there other men in your life?'

'Two I go out with occasionally at home. Separately, of course,' she added demurely.

Jack Spencer grinned, then sat back in his chair, his keen blue eyes challenging hers. 'Right. I now know a little about you. But you haven't asked me anything about myself. Does that mean you're not interested?'

'No.' She returned the look squarely. 'Just polite.'

He shrugged the impressive shoulders his suit jacket had obviously been custom-made to fit. 'In which case I'll supply answers to the questions you're too polite to ask.'

'You don't have to,' she said hurriedly, but he leaned forward, invading her space. 'I'm single, solvent, thirty-nine last birthday, and I build houses. That's about it.'

'And you're Abby's uncle,' she reminded him, as he sat back.

'True.' He raised a quizzical eyebrow. 'Does that help my case?'

'What case exactly?'

'I like you, Katharine Dysart.' He smiled crookedly. 'And I want you to like me. Do you?'

Kate stared at him for a moment. 'Are you always this direct?'

'No. I can be as devious as the next man when necessary,' he assured her. 'But where you're concerned I'm playing it straight. Will you have dinner with me tonight?'

Her eyes opened wide for a moment, then she began to laugh. 'Which question shall I answer first.'

'If you say yes to dinner I shall take it for granted you like me!' The blue eyes gleamed with amusement Kate found disarming. And she rather wished she could say yes.

'Sorry. I'm going out with a friend.'

'The college friend?'

'No. A different one.'

He thought for a moment. 'I'm involved in a working dinner tomorrow night. Thursday's the only evening I've got free otherwise. How does that suit you?'

'Sorry. I'm seeing Alasdair on Thursday.'

'Busy lady,' he said lightly, and fixed her with a steely blue look. 'Or are you just letting me down lightly, Miss Katharine Dysart?'

'Not at all. Friends call me Kate, by the way,' she added.

'Then so shall I.' He looked at his watch. 'Time up, Kate. I'll drive you back to Dysart's.'

After he'd negotiated the centre of town she directed him into the auction house car park just as Adam was emerging from his car, with eyebrows raised when he spotted his sister with a stranger.

'This one of the friends?' muttered Jack, as he retrieved Kate's bags from the back seat.

'No, my brother.' She called Adam over. 'Adam, this is Jack Spencer. Uncle of one of my pupils.'

The men shook hands, sizing each other up, and, to Kate's amusement, appeared to approve of what they saw.

'I must come along to one of your auctions some time,' said Jack after greetings were exchanged. 'I need some furniture in keeping with a cottage I'm doing up.'

'What period?' said Adam, interest caught at once.

'Early nineteenth century.'

'Come and have a browse round any time,' said Kate. 'Dad's the furniture man.'

'I'd be happy to,' said Jack, and handed over a pile of bags to Adam. 'Your sister's shopping. Good to have met you.' He turned to Kate. 'I hope I'll be luckier next time.'

She smiled. 'Thanks for the coffee.'

Adam watched the Jeep out into the street, then grabbed Kate by the elbow. 'What did he mean by that?'

'He wanted me to have dinner with him, but I'm going out tonight,' she said, shaking him off irritably. 'Preferably free of bruises.'

'What about Alasdair?' he demanded.

'What about him?'

'Is he your date for tonight?'

'No. I'm seeing him on Thursday. Tonight, just so you're completely up to date, I'm going out with Toby.' Kate grinned. 'Close your mouth, brother dear. Gaping doesn't suit you.'

'How long have you known this Spencer chap, then?' asked Adam, as they went inside.

'Since last Friday.'

'He seems pretty friendly after such a short time!'

'How long did you know Gabriel before you felt "friendly"?' she countered.

Adam paused outside his father's office, frowning. 'Are you serious about this man, then?'

'Not in the least. I'm not serious about Toby or Phil, either. Not even Alasdair.' Kate shook her head at him. 'I know this social whirl is a little unusual for a sober schoolmarm like me—'

'I don't think of you that way,' he said indignantly.

'No. But Fenny does. And she's right. So I've decided to turn over a new leaf and become a social butterfly instead!'

CHAPTER FIVE

FRANCES DYSART was astonished when she heard that in the short time since parting with her daughter Kate had not only managed to run into Jack Spencer, but have coffee with him at the Chesterton.

'Take her straight home, Frances,' said Tom Dysart, chuckling, 'or who knows what else she might get up to.'

Kate blew him a kiss, then asked her mother to drive on the way back to Stavely. 'Can't have Toby thinking I look like a hag tonight.'

'Where's he taking you? The Forrester's Arms? No, I suppose not, if you're going there with Alasdair on Thursday. How about tomorrow? Anyone lined up for that, or will you grace the family table?'

'Unless I get a better offer!'

'You should have let me buy you another dress for your dinner with Alasdair,' scolded Frances.

'The one I've got will do very well,' protested Kate. 'I'm told it's flattering.'

'Very flattering,' said her mother darkly. 'A good thing you're small.'

'If you mean it clings a bit, it's meant to.'

Frances sighed, impatient with herself. 'I'm an idiot. I worry that you lead too quiet a life in Foychurch, and now I'm fussing because your social life's gone up a gear. But Toby's an old friend, Alasdair too, so I don't have to worry about them.'

'Mother, you don't have to worry where Jack

Spencer's concerned either. Quite apart from the fact that he's related to one of my pupils, Adam liked him,' Kate reminded her.

'So he did,' said her mother, brightening, and overtook a heavy goods lorry with panache.

'How was Toby?' said Frances next day, over the lunch they'd invited Gabriel to share with them. 'Was it a good film?'

'Toby was the same as usual—pleasant, relaxing company—likewise the film.' Kate grinned at her mother. 'And, yes, he kissed me goodnight, and, no, I'm not seeing him again this half-term, but I probably shall when I'm home next.'

'I'm just interested,' said Frances, unrepentant, and held out her arms for her grandson. 'Alasdair rang last night, Kate. Said he couldn't get you on your cellphone.'

'I left it at home for once. What did he want?'

'Officially to confirm dinner with him tomorrow night. So he said.' Frances smiled smugly over the baby's head. 'But I think he just wanted a chat with you.'

'So what did you tell him?'

'That you were out with a friend. I asked if I could take a message, and he told me to say he'd call for you at seven tomorrow.'

Kate raised an eyebrow. 'We'd already arranged that.'

'Aha, he's keeping tabs on you. I hope you said Kate was with a *male* friend, Frances,' said Gabriel, laughing.

'I thought I'd better leave that to her!'

Kate glanced at Gabriel's heavy eyes. 'Tuck Hal up in his buggy and I'll take him for a stroll now it's cleared up a bit. Go home for a nap. Auntie'll take over for a couple of hours.'

Kate was very thoughtful, later, as she pushed the

buggy down a quiet lane in an afternoon bright with sunshine now rain had washed the snow away. She found it increasingly hard to believe in this new, persistent Alasdair who rang her so often. In their Cambridge days he'd treated her with affectionate indulgence, as though she were a clever child rather than an attractive female, with a full set of the normal feelings and needs that implied. Yet now that he apparently did see her as an attractive woman, she was no longer starry-eyed about him. Nor about any other man. Kate smiled down at the small sleeping face just visible above the covers in the buggy. Amazing that all men were as cute and helpless as this to start with. Even Alasdair.

This was hard to believe when Alasdair Drummond presented himself prompt at seven at Friars Wood the following evening. In a khaki crew neck sweater and black denims, a khaki reefer jacket hanging loose from his shoulders, he looked tall and tough and anything but helpless. Or cute.

'Hi. Are you ready, Kate?' He gave her the familiar bone-dissolving smile as she beckoned him inside.

'You're on time, Alasdair. Have a chat with my father while I get my coat.' She left him with Tom Dysart in the study and went to the kitchen, where her mother was humming along to the radio while she put the finishing touches to the evening meal.

'Alasdair's here,' Kate announced. 'He seems anxious to get going.'

Frances eyed her, frowning. 'I thought you were going to wear the gold dress again.'

Kate shook her head. 'It's cold, and the Forrester's is only a pub, no matter how good the food is, so I thought I'd be comfortable.'

In actual fact she *had* put the dress on at first, then

changed into jeans and a cinnamon wool sweater which clung even more than the dress. And instead of leaving her hair down she'd twisted it up securely, but with the odd curling tendril left to look as though it had escaped by accident.

'You look very pretty just the same,' conceded her mother. 'What coat are you wearing? Surely not the windbreaker you wear for school?'

'Why not?' said Kate carelessly. 'Come and say hello to Alasdair while I fetch it.'

'Did your mother tell you I rang the other night?' asked Alasdair, when they were on their way.

'Yes. I was out with a friend.'

'The man I saw at your place the other day?'

'No. A different friend. Son of my mother's bosom pal. Toby's the junior partner with a firm of local accountants.'

Alasdair drove in silence for a while, then cast a frowning glance in her direction. 'Harking back to the man I ran into at your place—you said he was important. How important?'

'I don't know yet. I haven't known him long.'

'Has Adam met him?'

'Yes.'

'Does he approve?'

Kate gave him a hostile glance. 'It doesn't matter whether Adam approves of Jack Spencer or not, but as it happens he does.'

'So why didn't you ask the man along on Sunday?'

'Because it was a family thing.'

'*I* was there,' Alasdair pointed out.

'Not by my invitation.'

He threw a hostile glance at her. 'I'm beginning to think this was a mistake.'

'We could always turn back.'

'Is that what you want?'

She shrugged. 'Not particularly. I'll have missed dinner by now.'

'So you'll bear with my company as long as I provide you with food?' he said with sarcasm.

Kate felt sudden contrition. 'Alasdair, if I've been unfriendly I'm sorry. But last time we met—by which I mean years ago, when you wiped the floor with me for wasting my so-called talents—we parted on bad terms. Did you really expect me to welcome you with open arms when you turned up again out of the blue?'

'If I did I was out of luck,' he said morosely, and sighed. 'Look, Kate, I miscalculated by turning up at your school last week without warning. I know I should have got in touch first, but I was feeling pretty low after my grandmother's funeral. There was an early hotel lunch for the mourners afterwards so my parents could drive back to Scotland straight after it. I couldn't face the empty house on my own for a while, so on impulse I drove to see you.'

'And got a cold shoulder for your pains,' said Kate wryly.

'You could say that. There's a sign ahead,' he added. 'Do I turn here?'

'Yes. The pub is a little way down on the right.'

The Forrester's Arms was popular, and Alasdair had to nudge his way through the crowded bar to clear a way for Kate. She waved at several familiar faces, then in response to a beckoning hand took Alasdair over to meet Chris and Jane Morgan, from the farm near Friars Wood.

'Squeeze in here with us. We're going in for a meal shortly,' said Chris. 'How are you, Kate?'

'Fine,' she said, smiling, and introduced Alasdair. 'Adam recommended this place, but I didn't know it was so busy mid-week.'

'It's the new chef—his way with pastry is out of this world,' said Jane, smiling at Alasdair. 'I hope you booked.'

He confirmed that he had, then went off to buy drinks, leaving Kate to answer questions about the newest Dysart arrival for a while.

'So is this Alasdair the current boyfriend?' asked Chris, with the familiarity of someone who'd known Kate all her life.

'Friend, not boyfriend,' she corrected. 'We were students together for a while, back in the mists of time.'

'Listen to the old lady,' mocked Jane, eyeing Alasdair's back view with approval. '*Very* nice, Kate. Ah! Mrs Jennings is waving a menu at us, Chris. Our dinner must be ready.'

Her large husband leapt up with alacrity. 'Great, I'm starving. Nice to see you, Kate.'

'You, too. Thanks for your table.' Left to herself, Kate gazed into space for a while, deep in thought, and decided it was time to change her attitude towards Alasdair. She could have said no to the evening, she knew very well. But because she had agreed to it she might as well be civil, if only in return for the money he was laying out on her meal.

A young girl rushed up with a menu, and explained that because they were so crowded it might be a while before they were actually served with their meal.

'Dinner may be a little late,' Kate informed Alasdair when he joined her.

He handed her a glass of something long and ice-filled, and sat down beside her to drink his beer.

'I can see why; it's like a rugby scrum at the bar!' He cast an eye at the menu she was studying. 'Maybe you should choose something *en croûte*, if the chef is a genius with pastry. There's no alcohol hiding in that, by the way,' he added, indicating her glass. 'Just fruit juice and lemonade.'

'I'm not averse to alcohol, Alasdair. Just wine.'

'You used to drink a glass or two now and then in the old days.'

She shrugged. 'I've changed since then.'

He gave her a wintry look. 'Damn right you have. I just wish I knew why you'd changed so much towards *me*. We got on well together once.'

She smiled. 'I grew up.'

'So you keep telling me.' Alasdair applied himself to the menu again. 'I think it's the Gressingham duck for me.'

'I'll have the bacon and egg pie,' she announced, and giggled at his look of astonishment. 'Why not? I like that kind of thing.'

After Alasdair had given the rushed little waitress their order he leaned back in his seat, eyeing Kate challengingly. 'So. Do I detect a slight thaw in the atmosphere?'

'Yes.' She gave him a friendly smile. 'I keep telling you I've grown up, so it's time I started behaving that way. Tell me about your new job.'

He looked down his nose at her. 'You don't have to be polite just because I'm buying dinner.'

'I'm interested. I really want to know.' she assured him, and listened, fascinated, while Alasdair described his job with Healthshield, and told her that the pharmaceutical international had appointed him as operations director of their new UK branch after his successful research into a mania-controlling drug.

'So I wasn't far out about a miracle cure,' said Kate, impressed.

'It's not a cure,' he said quickly. 'But if my brainchild merely improves life in certain cases I'll feel I've done something worthwhile.'

'I'll drink to that.' She raised her glass to him.

'By the way,' said Alasdair casually, 'the man I met at your place—what does he do for a living?'

'Jack? He's a builder.'

Alasdair looked taken aback. 'Oh, right. What does he build?'

'Houses.'

Alasdair grinned. 'He builds houses and his name is Jack?'

Kate laughed. 'I hadn't thought of that.'

The lighter mood prevailed as they did justice to the meal, and for the first time since they'd met again they began to talk with the ease of old. As the evening progressed Kate thought they might almost have been the two students from the past. This time, however, there was one great difference. Alasdair was making it clear he found her desirable, and, though the less cerebral side of her liked that—and Kate had to admit she found him more physically attractive than ever—she was no longer desperately in love with him. Which made things a great deal more comfortable all round, she thought with satisfaction.

'So where did you go the other night?' asked Alasdair, over the coffee they'd elected to drink at the table rather than fight for a place back in the bar.

'To Bristol for a meal and a trip to the cinema.'

He frowned. 'But it snowed like the devil. It must have been tricky driving back.'

'We made it across the Severn Bridge safely enough in Toby's four-wheel drive. And as usual Adam was lurking when we arrived, to make sure little sister got home in one piece.' Kate wagged an admonishing finger. 'So don't you start, Alasdair. One brother's more than enough.'

The grey eyes lit with an unholy gleam. 'Believe me, Katharine Dysart, the last thing I feel towards you is brotherly.'

'You did once.'

'Ah, yes. But, as you've taken pains to point out to me so often, you've grown up since then.' He smiled. 'You were a clever, skinny little kid in the old days, all eyes and hair. You're a woman now, Kate, and a good-looking one at that. But, just as it was back then, half your appeal for me is the brain behind those gold cat's eyes of yours.'

'Cat's eyes!'

'A sexy Persian cat,' he assured her, and stood up to hold her chair for her.

The precarious rapport between them held on the journey back right up to the point when Alasdair startled his passenger by turning in to a layby a couple of miles short of Friars Wood. They were out in the country on a minor road with no streetlights, no other houses in view, and at this time of night no traffic passing by—a factor which won Alasdair a look of dark suspicion from Kate.

'Why have we stopped?' she demanded.

He undid his seatbelt, then reached over and undid hers. 'Don't be naive,' he said, and kissed her.

Kate's immediate reaction was a sense of disbelief. This was Alasdair, she had to remind herself. This really was happening. And, instead of pulling away, she decided she might as well savour the sensation as Alasdair's lips parted hers. If only out of curiosity. She made no protest even when he pulled her as close as it was possible to manage in the confines of the car, but when his mouth seduced hers with a sudden savagery unexpected heat shot through her, and she gasped as his hands pushed her jacket aside to caress her breasts through the thin sweater.

Despite the leap in her blood Kate's principal sensation was heady elation at the knowledge that Alasdair wanted her. Her, Kate, at last. To be here in his arms like this was something she'd dreamed of once, fantasised over. But in the past her dreams had only been of her own part in the process. It had never occurred to her that Alasdair's reaction would be so intense.

He tore his mouth away at last and thrust his hands in her hair, bringing it tumbling down in a black cascade over the white of her jacket as he stared at her in the darkness. 'I must have been blind,' he said hoarsely.

Kate gazed up at him in silence he very plainly found unnerving.

'Aren't you going to ask when?' he demanded.

She reached up to remove his hands so she could push her hair back behind her ears. 'I know when. You mean in the old days at Trinity, when I was so madly in love with you.'

'Were you, Kate?' he said caressingly, and kissed her again, but this time she pushed him away.

'Of course I was. But that was a long time ago.'

He subsided behind the wheel and stared out into the darkness, the ragged rhythm of his breathing deeply satisfying to Kate.

'So tell me the truth, Alasdair,' she said, breaking a

prolonged, hostile silence. 'And no nonsense about impulses, please.'

'What do you mean?' he said brusquely, turning towards her.

'Why *did* you turn up in Foychurch last week?'

'I told you. Adam had told me where you teach, so it seemed the most natural thing in the world to drive there and look you up.' He shrugged. 'I was fool enough to want to surprise you.'

'You certainly managed that. But why, Alasdair? It's years since there was any contact between us. It seems so odd to me that you actually drove to Foychurch, when a phone call would have done just as well.'

Kate sat patiently during another silence, waiting for Alasdair to speak. When he did his voice was tinged with the Edinburgh accent which only manifested itself in times of anger or stress.

'All right,' he said at last. 'I admit I was curious. You know I had lunch with Adam recently? Naturally enough, the conversation turned to you. I've always liked your brother—'

'The feeling's mutual,' she assured him dryly.

'Because of that Adam felt able to talk to me about something close to his heart. And afterwards it preyed on my mind.'

Kate stared at him. 'What on earth did he say?'

Alasdair leaned closer. 'He asked me if I knew what the hell had happened to cause the change in you when we were up at Trinity together.'

She turned away to stare through the windscreen at a watery moon breaking through the clouds. 'And what did you tell him?'

'That I had no idea. You suddenly shut yourself away from everyone, including me, saying you'd fallen behind with your work.' Alasdair kept his eyes fixed on her profile. 'But Adam said something went very wrong with your life before you came home that summer. He hoped I might have some clue as to what happened to make you so jumpy and withdrawn. Apparently it took a long holiday in Italy with Jess before you returned to anything like normal.' He sighed heavily. 'Since talking to Adam, I keep wondering if I was to blame.'

'You most definitely were not,' she said emphatically, and turned towards him. 'I admit I had an outsize crush on you. But my heart wasn't broken, Alasdair. I managed to survive the rest of my time at Cambridge perfectly well without you—even achieved a reasonable degree,' she added with sarcasm.

'I know your work wasn't affected,' he agreed. 'And your degree was brilliant, not just reasonable. Which is why I can never understand—'

'If you mention one word about my job again, Alasdair, I shall get out and walk home. Now.'

'All right, all right!' He took her hand. 'But Adam started much racking of brains on my part. I kept trying to figure out how I could have unknowingly done something to hurt you, Kate. So when he invited me to the christening I just had to see you first, to find out if I'd been responsible for—'

'Oh, I see! You came to Foychurch to seek absolution for a sin you weren't even sure you'd committed.' She removed her hand to pat his. 'Don't worry, Alasdair. You didn't ruin my life. In fact I like it very much just the way it is.'

'If you say so,' he said, with such obvious doubt Kate was amused.

'Not all of us are cut out for high-flying careers like yours, Alasdair Drummond. Jack Spencer, for instance, is obviously perfectly comfortable with his job in the building trade. He doesn't have to be part of a global empire to feel he's doing something worthwhile. Nor,' she added significantly, 'do I.'

'So Adam's imagining things where you're concerned.' commented Alasdair, pointedly ignoring the reference to Jack Spencer.

'Yes. But not so much these days, thank heavens, since he's been married to Gabriel. Now, can we change the subject, please?'

'Whatever you say.' He put out a hand to touch hers. 'Kate, it's been good just to be with you again tonight, but I want more of your time than this. How about taking the train to Pennington on Saturday to have lunch with me? Please,' he added deliberately.

Kate thought about it, quite gratified by Alasdair in the role of supplicant. And, because she had nothing planned for Saturday, decided there was no harm in seeing him again before she went back to her quiet life in Foychurch. 'All right,' she said at last. 'But no train. I'll drive.'

'And what if it snows?' he demanded.

'I can sleep on the couch in Dad's office. Or,' she added, giving him a cheeky little grin, 'you can take me home to Gloucester and put me up in your spare room.'

Alasdair gave a crack of laughter. 'You trust me enough for that?'

'Of course. Otherwise,' she added, 'the deal's off.'

'In other words I'm to keep my hands to myself.' He sighed theatrically. 'A tall order, Kate.'

'Oh, for heaven's sake,' she said irritably. 'If you're referring to what happened between us just now, that was just a kiss between old friends—' The rest of her sentence was smothered by a kiss which had so little to

do with friendship it silenced them both very effectively.
It was a long time before Alasdair released her. And
when he did it was with a reluctance which did more
for Kate's ego than she cared to let him see.

'I suppose now,' he said huskily, 'you're going to
change your mind about seeing me again.'

If she were sensible, yes. But knowing that Alasdair
wanted her added an element of risk Kate was far too
human not to enjoy. She pretended to think it over, then
shrugged carelessly. 'I haven't anything planned for
Saturday, so I might as well come. But I'll have to get
back early.'

Saturday dawned fine, with no sign of snow. Well aware
that she had the blessing of the entire Dysart family behind her, Kate drove off to Pennington during the morning, knowing that even if the worst happened, and she
were obliged to stay the night in Alasdair's house, none
of them would worry in the slightest—Adam least of all.
Kate grinned to herself as she sped along the A48. Little
did they know that Alasdair was as prone to basic urges
as the next man where she was concerned. It had done
her morale no end of good to know that only the sheer
physical difficulty of making love in his Maserati had
prevented him from trying to take things a lot further
during the episode in the layby. Which meant that he
might expect more than that in more favourable circumstances.

It was not a thought that worried her. She liked
Alasdair's lovemaking. Liked it all the more in some
perverse way because it was easier to enjoy now that
she was no longer crazy about him. But, astonishingly
passionate though he'd been the other night, she was
sure that the slightest hint of protest from her would have

been enough to call a halt, even if they'd been somewhere more private. Like his house in Gloucester. A prospect she rather fancied, if only out of curiosity to see where he lived.

Thoughts of Alasdair's home led her to wondering about Jack Spencer's. His house was in bad repair, by the sound of it, if it needed doing up. But in his line of business no doubt he'd bought it for a song, relying on his own skill to save him expensive labour costs.

When she got to Pennington Kate found Alasdair's unmistakable Maserati already in the auction house car park, and its owner in the office with Adam in a conversation which broke off abruptly at the sight of her, his eyes igniting with a heat Kate responded to with a friendly smile.

'Morning, Alasdair,' she said cheerfully, and frowned at her brother's dark-circled eyes in sympathy. 'Oh, dear. Bad night?'

Adam smiled wryly. 'My turn for the two o'clock feed. The little demon took ages to get back to sleep afterwards.'

'The joys of fatherhood,' she said with mock sympathy.

'I'm not complaining—at least not much,' he said, and grinned at Alasdair. 'You should try it.'

'I hope to, one day,' Alasdair assured him, and turned to Kate. 'On Adam's recommendation I booked lunch at a French restaurant down the road.'

'Wonderful. School dinners will take some getting used to when I go back!' She smiled at Adam. 'Why not join us?'

'No, thanks. I'm saving myself for dinner tonight. Mother's looking after Hal, and I'm taking Gabriel out for the first time since the son and heir arrived. By the way,' he added, 'your friend called in this morning, Kate. I gave him a sneak preview of the furniture in next week's auction.'

'Jack Spencer?' she said, surprised. 'Did he see anything he fancied?'

'Quite a bit,' Adam grinned at Alasdair. 'I showed him some of your stuff, but no luck.'

Alasdair shrugged. 'Depends on taste, I suppose.'

'What kind of thing was he after?' asked Kate, amused by the idea of Jack Spencer turning up his nose at Alasdair's cast-offs.

'He was very keen on a little mahogany side table, circa 1800—asked me to look out for pieces of the same period. He fancied a Cartier brooch, too.'

'Time we were off, Kate,' said Alasdair abruptly, and held the door open for her. 'See you, Adam.'

'You were in a hurry,' commented Kate as they walked down the Parade towards the restaurant.

'I was keen to get you to myself,' he informed her. 'Full marks to Adam for his tact in refusing to come with us.'

'You lunched with him at the Chesterton, which is more than I'm getting,' she pointed out. 'Not, of course, that I object to your choice for today.'

'Glad to hear it. Though we can eat at the Chesterton if you prefer.'

'No way. Too expensive. I had coffee there the other day with Jack.'

'Ah, yes. The builder with expensive tastes.'

Kate looked up at him in amusement. Alasdair was wearing a steel-grey moleskin suit the colour of his eyes, which were wintry as he strode along at a pace too fast for comfort for his companion.

'Slow *down*, Alasdair,' she protested. 'It's only just after midday.'

'Sorry,' he said shortly, and matched his stride to hers.

She frowned. 'Why were you getting steamed up about Jack's taste in furniture?'

'Not furniture. Women. Or one woman, to be exact. Who is the Cartier brooch intended for, I wonder?' Alasdair stopped dead under one of the leafless trees in the middle of the broad pavement. He seized her hands, oblivious of passers-by. 'Tell me the truth. Are you serious about this man, Kate?'

She stared at him angrily. 'Not that it's any business of yours, Alasdair, but the answer's no. I'm not committed to anyone else, either. Now, for heaven's sake let me go. We're attracting attention.'

Alasdair kept one of her hands in his as they made for the restaurant. 'So what's wrong with commitment?'

'Nothing. For those who care for it.'

'But you don't. Why?'

Kate eyed him with exasperation. 'Let's change the subject or I won't enjoy my lunch.'

She didn't enjoy her lunch anyway, because the first person they saw, sitting alone at a table the waiter led them past, was Jack Spencer.

CHAPTER SIX

JACK looked up from the newspaper he was reading and jumped to his feet, his pleasure immediate at the sight of her.

'Why, he*llo*, Kate. Adam didn't say you'd be here when he recommended this place.'

'Hello yourself, Jack. Adam mentioned that you'd been in Dysart's this morning.' Kate smiled at him brightly, resolving to do her brother an injury the first opportunity she got. 'Let me introduce you. Alasdair Drummond—Jack Spencer.'

Alasdair shook the other man's hand with such cold courtesy that, after a brief enquiry to Jack about the new baby, Kate said goodbye and accompanied Alasdair to the table he'd booked for the lunch she no longer wanted.

'Does Adam get a commission on the number of customers he introduces here?' muttered Alasdair, holding her chair for her.

'It's a subject I'll take up with him as soon as I get home,' promised Kate, amused when Alasdair seated her very deliberately with her back to Jack Spencer.

'Does your friend live in Pennington?' he asked.

'No.'

'Where, then?'

'I don't know, exactly. I haven't known him long. And, unlike you,' she said, scowling at him, 'I don't subject my friends to inquisitions.'

Kate studied her menu in pointed, brooding silence, then asked for mineral water.

'You should have come by train and enjoyed a glass of wine,' said Alasdair.

'I don't drink wine,' she said shortly. 'I'm not very hungry either, Alasdair. Could I just have soup, please?'

'Anything you like,' he said promptly, the ice melting in his eyes. 'What would you like to do after lunch?'

'What do you suggest?'

'I'll think of something while we eat,' he promised.

Halfway through their meal Alasdair told her to look round. 'Your friend is leaving.'

Kate turned in her chair, smiled in answer to Jack's farewell wave, then returned to her soup with more enthusiasm.

'You can relax now,' said Alasdair, and gave her a wry look. 'Your friend was a lot more delighted at the sight of you than I would have been in the same circumstances.'

'Because I was with you?' Kate shrugged. 'He's just a friend, Alasdair.'

'And is that how you refer to me?'

She smiled sweetly. 'If you mean in conversation with Jack—or anyone else—I have to confess that I don't refer to you at all.'

Alasdair sighed in mock sorrow. 'You certainly know how to deflate a man's ego, Kate.'

She laughed suddenly. 'Sorry, Alasdair. Our farewell lunch hasn't been much of a success, has it?'

'Farewell?' he said, frowning.

She nodded. 'School starts on Monday. I'm driving back to Foychurch tomorrow.'

'It's not on another planet,' he pointed out. 'I've got a week or so to go yet before I actually take over at the

Healthshield plant. After the distances I travelled in the States, the journey to Foychurch for an evening is nothing.'

Kate eyed him narrowly. 'What *is* all this, Alasdair? You've managed perfectly well without my company all these years. Why this sudden yen for it now?'

He was silent for a moment, then smiled wryly. 'I could say I'm feeling low because my grandmother died, that I don't know anyone in Gloucester any more, that my friends are based in Edinburgh or the US. All of which is true enough.' His eyes held hers. 'But even if I were surrounded by people clamouring for my company, now that I've caught up with you again I prefer to spend time with you, Kate. Is that so hard to believe?'

'Of course it is,' she said impatiently.

'Then I must find a way to convince you. So, if you've finished playing with that soup, let's have some coffee, and afterwards we'll go shopping.'

Kate's eyebrows rose. 'Shopping?'

He smiled. 'For food. Lunch was such a dismal failure I'm inviting you home to tea, Miss Dysart. Choose what you want to eat first, then we'll drive to my place in Gloucester and you can give me some advice on interior decoration. After which you can leave for home as early as you want. And if you're worried that I'll expect to take up where I left off in the car the other night, I promise, hand on heart, to restrain myself. So will you come?'

The plates had been removed and coffee provided before Kate answered him. 'All right. As long as you don't take consent for anything other than curiosity to see your house,' she said bluntly.

'You used to trust me once,' he reminded her.

She gave him a bleak little smile. 'Sad to say, I har-
bour less illusions these days. Even about you.'

Certain that the Maserati would outstrip her modest little
car, no matter how hard Alasdair tried to hold back, Kate
asked for directions to his house before following him
to the outskirts of Gloucester. Relieved that she hadn't
been obliged to negotiate the town itself, she wasn't long
behind Adam when she finally arrived in a cul-de-sac
that brought her to End House, the name carved on stone
gateposts. She turned through them into a short drive
which led past herbaceous borders, and parked beside
the Maserati on the neatly raked gravel which encircled
the lawn in front of the house.

When Alasdair came to help her out Kate asked for
time to look at the outside before going in.

'The main part is late eighteenth century,' he told her,
'but the double frontage is early Victorian. These huge
bay windows would have been the latest fashion when
they were added.'

Alasdair unlocked a wide oak door to reveal an inner
white-painted door with stained glass panels. He opened
it with a flourish, and switched on lights to reveal a long
hallway with a beautiful wood floor and a staircase
which curved up at the far end. Alasdair led her past
tantalising glimpses of rooms through half-open doors,
straight to a big kitchen with a stone-flagged floor and
an original black-leaded range in perfect keeping with
the pine dresser which took up one entire wall.

'The range still works, but isn't in use any more,' he
explained, switching on a kettle. 'Hence the electric
cooker alongside it.'

'What a great kitchen!' said Kate, admiring an as-
sortment of windsor chairs grouped round a large

scrubbed-top table. 'You won't change anything in here, surely?'

'Only the colour of the walls. Through that door there's a larder that houses my brand new dishwasher, laundry equipment and man-size fridge-freezer.' He grinned as he took a teapot and cups from the dresser. 'I like my creature comforts.' While Kate examined her surroundings he made tea, put some pastries on a large plate, then with a mocking bow took a blue ceramic vase of daffodils from a window ledge and placed it in the centre of the table. 'Can't let myself be outdone by your builder friend.'

Kate's eyes narrowed at the pejorative hint in his tone. 'I wouldn't have put you down as a snob, Alasdair.'

To her astonishment he looked discomfited. 'I'm not. I couldn't care less what the guy does for a living. My gripe comes from the fact that he's your "friend".'

'But not the only one,' she reminded him tartly. 'I can also notch up an accountant and a teacher. Though Phil Dent is slightly up the scale from me in your eyes, I suppose, because he teaches at an expensive boys' school.'

Alasdair put down a milk jug with a force that spilt some of its contents on the table. 'For the last time, Kate I do *not* look down on your profession. At any level. I'm sure that you, and all your colleagues, do a fantastic and vital job. But you know as well as I do that you hadn't the least intention of teaching when you were at Trinity. Have you forgotten that I was the one you confided in? All those dreams about being part of some record-breaking research programme—'

'I was a starry-eyed kid,' said Kate dismissively, and poured tea.

'So you were.' He smiled, and put a miniature coffee tart on her plate like a peace offering.

She eyed it absently for a moment, then looked up at him. 'Shortly before you left to take on the big wide world, Alasdair, I experienced a kind of epiphany. I discovered I no longer cared tuppence that someone had beaten me to it about the discovery of DNA and so on. Dreamtime was over.' She shrugged. 'Reality was as respectable a degree as possible, followed by a teacher-training course.'

'Your degree was a hell of a sight more than respectable.'

She picked up the tart. 'Can we please talk about something else?'

'Paint,' he said promptly.

Kate chuckled. 'Safe subject!'

'What colour should I have in here? I'd thought maybe some kind of blue.'

She shook her head. 'Too cold against this floor. You need something warm, like terracotta—even red.'

Alasdair eyed his kitchen walls for a moment, then nodded. 'You're right. I'll show you some colour cards later. If you've finished your tea, do you fancy a tour?'

Kate jumped up with alacrity. 'Lead on.'

Because Alasdair had dispensed with some of the house's contents she had expected a forlorn air to the rooms he showed her, but the small sitting room was cosy, with leather chairs and velvet cushions, and in the drawing room there were big sofas with plain cream covers. In the square bay window, with its view of the garden, there was a gilded bergere sofa that would have brought a gleam to Tom Dysart's eye.

Kate raised her eyebrows. 'This is all a surprise, Alasdair—I thought you'd evicted the furniture?'

He shook his head. 'Only the pieces I didn't like. And a fair amount of clutter. While my parents were here we went through the house together. As you see, I've kept a few pictures and pieces of silver and so on, but with my mother's approval out went a chaise covered with horsehair which pricked like blazes, and tables and cabinets and whatnots of every description. The dining room had a gigantic mahogany sideboard with a mirror which only stopped short of the ceiling, while upstairs you couldn't move for wardrobes and chests.'

'But what will you use instead?' asked Kate, following him up the curving staircase.

'I've kept this wardrobe for myself until I get some cupboards built.' Alasdair ushered her into what was obviously the master bedroom, where a large bed kept company with an equally large wardrobe. 'Fortunately I was able to hang on to the bed, because my grandfather was built on the same scale as me.' He waved a hand at a door across the room. 'I'll get a shower fitted in the dressing room in there, modernise the main bathroom, and add another to one of the other bedrooms while I'm at it. My forebears may have considered one bathroom sufficient for the entire household, but from a resale point of view that's not on.'

'Are you doing the house up just to sell it, then?'

Alasdair shrugged. 'I'll have to see how things work out.'

'This is a lovely house,' Kate assured him, as he showed her the rest of it. 'You wouldn't have much trouble in selling it.'

'But it's a lot of house to live in alone. It's meant for a large family, which is something, oddly enough, that it's never achieved. My mother was an only child, which is how I came to inherit it.'

'She didn't want to live here?'

He shook his head. 'Neither of my parents has the least desire to leave Edinburgh. In the beginning my mother brought me down here in the school holidays, but when I was old enough I came on my own. I went fishing with my grandfather, helped my grandmother with the garden, and the nearest neighbours had a grandson I hobnobbed with very happily. I always felt at home here.'

'I can understand why,' Kate assured him.

Alasdair took her by the hand and led her downstairs. 'Enough nostalgia. Now you've had a quick survey, let's think about paint again.'

In the kitchen Kate asked for paper, and sat down at the table to sketch a room plan. 'You've got to live here,' she reminded him, studying shade cards. 'I tend to choose primary colours, but maybe you'd prefer something more muted.'

'I like the gold walls in your little doll's house,' said Alasdair, sitting beside her.

'Compact, not little! And the colour's Maize Glow in brochure-speak. I tend to go for sunny colours. My bedroom's done in something called Ripe Apricot.'

'I'd like to see it,' he said, and smiled blandly. 'Purely as research, of course, to help with my decorating.'

'Not that you need pale colours here,' said Kate, ignoring him. 'The windows let in so much light you can do anything you like in rooms this size.'

Eventually, after two or three choices had been pencilled in for each room, Alasdair told her that there was still a week to go before his official appointment to the new post.

'I'll go in for an hour or two on a couple of days, to meet people and familiarise myself with the set-up. But

I start in earnest on Monday week.' He looked at his watch. 'So what time do you want to start back for Stavely this evening, Kate?'

'Pretty soon, I'm afraid.'

He frowned. 'Do you have to?'

She thought about it. 'I don't *have* to, I suppose.'

'Then stay for dinner. I'll cook.'

Kate smiled. 'An offer I can't refuse. I like it when men cook for me.'

'Does it happen a lot then?' he said, amused.

'Phil, the sports teacher, fancies himself as a chef, but Toby, the accountant, prefers to eat out.'

'And Jack the builder? Is he a star in the kitchen, too?'

'If he is he hasn't said so,' said Kate truthfully.

Alasdair gave her a searching look. 'It seems to me that you must favour one of these ''friends'' more than the others?'

'If I did,' she said tartly, 'there would be *only* one.'

'But if you had to choose between one of them, who would it be?'

'Why do you want to know?'

'You know bloody well why,' he said with a sudden violence, and got up. 'Let's go for a stroll round the garden before the light goes.'

Kate slid her arms into the jacket he held for her, pleased that Alasdair was angry with her for having more than one man in her life. Or even other men besides him, maybe. Though why he should have expected otherwise after all this time was hard to imagine. It wasn't like him to be so illogical, she thought with amusement, as they strolled past neatly trimmed lawns and beds full of spring flowers about to burst into colour.

'It's a lovely afternoon,' she said after a while, to break the brooding silence between them.

'I wish it wasn't,' he said morosely. 'I hoped it would snow. I'd rather you slept in one of the spare rooms than drive back to Stavely late tonight.'

'It's not going to be late,' she informed him. 'I'm leaving straight after dinner.'

'My point exactly. And tomorrow you're leaving for Foychurch—and who knows when I'll see you again?'

Kate halted, eyeing him challengingly. 'Alasdair, I just can't get to grips with this new enthusiasm for my company. It's years since I even thought about you much, and don't tell me you've thought about me, either. If at all. Because I refuse to believe it.'

He stared down at her sombrely for a moment, then shrugged. 'All right. If you want the truth, it was only when I came back here that I started thinking of you again. Even before I caught up with Adam. Just being in the house here again brought back that Christmas when you invited me over to supper at Friars Wood. Because you were afraid I'd be lonely. I remembered what a sweet kid you were, and realised that I'd cared about you more than I knew. Suddenly I wanted to know how you were now, what had happened to you since I saw you last. Getting in touch with Adam wasn't solely about furniture, Kate.'

'And Adam, it seems, gave you the impression that I've been eating my heart out for you all these years! That must have pleased your male ego, Alasdair.'

'It wasn't like that,' he said flatly, as they resumed their walk. 'You know Adam's always been protective about you.'

Kate smiled wryly. 'You don't know the half of it. He was furious because I invited you over that Christmas. He was convinced you were some hunk lusting after my body.'

Alasdair let out a crack of laughter. 'Whereas I was about the only male in your vicinity who wasn't!'

'Don't rub it in! I knew that only too well.' She sighed theatrically. 'Sad, really, when I was so desperately in love with you.'

'Were you really, Kate?' he said softly, and came to a halt to look down at her. 'So what did I do to turn you against me?'

'Nothing, Alasdair. You did nothing at all.' She said it so flatly sudden comprehension gleamed in his eyes.

'I *see*. You would have preferred me to lust after you like the rest?'

Kate shook her head. 'No way. I wanted you to be in *love* with me. Lust wasn't something I knew much about at the time.'

'But you've learned since?'

'What do you expect? I'm a teacher, not a nun!'

He laughed, and took her hand in his. 'So if Adam objected to my presence, why was he so friendly when I turned up that Christmas?'

'Because you were older than either of us, and very obviously not lusting after me at all. He took one look and decided you were one of the good guys.' Kate smiled at him. 'But you worried my sisters no end.'

He turned a surprised look on her. 'How did I manage that?'

'By being immune to my youthful charms when I was so obviously bowled over by yours. They never discussed it with me, of course,' she assured him. 'But I knew they were worried. I think Leo still is.'

Alasdair stopped dead. 'Why should she be worried?'

'Leo wants everyone to live happily ever after, like she does with Jonah.'

'And she obviously thinks there's no chance of that for you where I'm concerned?'

'Right.' Kate shivered suddenly, and Alasdair took her hand.

'You're cold. Let's go inside.'

'What are you going to cook for me?' she asked, as they went back into the warm kitchen.

'Steak and salad do you?' he asked, taking her jacket.

'Perfect. What can I do to help?'

'Just sit there and look decorative while I slave over a hot stove. How about a drink?' he added.

'Do you have brandy?'

'Finest French cognac,' he assured her.

'Ginger ale?'

'That too.'

Kate grinned. 'Then I'll have a teaspoon of your cognac in a tall glass of ginger ale.'

When Alasdair came back from the larder with her drink, and a beer for himself, Kate sipped at hers while she watched him switch on the grill and season a pair of steaks.

'I can make the salad,' she offered, but he shook his head.

'Just sit there and talk to me.' He looked up with a gleam in his eye. 'You can do the cooking when I come to your doll's house.'

Kate gave that some thought, not at all sure she wanted her life in Foychurch disrupted by visits from Alasdair Drummond. Or from anyone else, Jack Spencer included. As she'd told Alasdair, the village was a close-knit community, where everyone had accepted her from the first. Consequently she'd always kept her socialising where men were concerned in Stavely, to save complications.

'I hesitate to cast a blight over the evening,' she said, with a sigh, 'but I don't think visits to Foychurch are a good idea.'

'That's obvious,' he said shortly, and gave her a tablecloth and a handful of silverware. 'Lay the table while you explain why.'

Kate did her best, but she could see she was making no headway. 'I prefer to keep my life there separate,' she finished lamely. 'It's easier that way.'

'Why?' Alasdair's tone was caustic. 'Was a vow of chastity required when you were taken on at the school?'

She laughed. 'No, of course not.'

'Then what's the harm in seeing an old friend like me once in a while? Lord knows it won't be often once I'm involved in the new job.' He turned on her suddenly. 'Why me, anyway? This embargo obviously doesn't apply to your friend Jack.'

'The day you saw him he was just bringing flowers to thank me for looking after his niece.'

'Have you seen him since? Other than today, I mean?'

'Yes' she admitted reluctantly.

'And did he ask to see you again?'

'Yes.'

Alasdair sliced a cucumber with a speed and violence Kate watched with trepidation. 'In this idyllic community you like so much, an old friend like me must surely cause less comment than the uncle of one of your pupils? You could be accused of favouritism every time you give his niece a gold star or whatever,' he pointed out, and rammed the steak under the grill.

'Oh, all right, Alasdair,' she said irritably. 'You've made your point.'

'Then I rest my case. How rare do you like your steak?'

Once they'd sat down Kate set out to defuse the situation by discussing Alasdair's work again, a subject as dear to his heart as it was fascinating to her. Consequently the meal was more of a success than had seemed possible at one point.

Due to her informed, intelligent questions he expanded at length, then stopped short at last, eyeing her in apology.

'I tend to get carried away. You're a very good listener.'

'I find it fascinating,' she assured him.

'Which is why I'll never understand—' He stopped, shaking his head. 'No, I won't go there again.'

After the meal Alasdair put a match to the logs in the drawing room fireplace.

'You needn't have done that,' said Kate. 'I can't stay long.'

'At least you'll go home warm.'

'The heating here is very efficient for such a big house. I wouldn't have thought you'd need a fire as well.'

'I told you I like my creature comforts.' He sat beside her on a sofa he'd pulled nearer the fire, and turned to her with a look which made Kate faintly uneasy. 'So. If I'm forbidden to visit you in Foychurch, do I have to wait until Easter to see you again?'

Kate gazed into the crackling fire, suddenly feeling rather silly. This was the twenty-first century, she reminded herself. Probably no one in the village had the least interest in her social life. 'All right. If you want to come to Foychurch you can,' she said at last. 'But you'd have to leave at a respectable hour.'

'To safeguard your reputation?'

'No,' she said impatiently. 'So I can get a good night's sleep. I get up early during the week.'

Alasdair took her hand. 'Are you actually saying I can come calling, Miss Dysart?'

She turned on him sharply. 'I'm actually saying that you can come round one night next week if you like, Alasdair.'

'But I am not to read anything more than that into it?'

'There isn't any more,' she said flatly.

'Oh, yes, there is,' he assured her, and pulled her onto his lap. He looked down into her startled face for a moment, then lowered his head to kiss her, his arms closing round her like a vice.

CHAPTER SEVEN

KATE stiffened in protest, and after a moment Alasdair relaxed his arms a little and moved his mouth away from hers.

'You said you wouldn't take up where we left off,' she accused.

'I'm not. I'm starting from the beginning again. Only this time,' he whispered, his breath hot against her cheek, 'we're not in a car, on a cold, dark road, but here on my home turf, in warmth and complete privacy—an arrangement I like a lot better.' His lips grazed her earlobe. 'I like the feel of you in my arms even more.'

And the hell of it was, thought Kate, that she did, too. She turned her head away. 'It's my own fault. Just by coming here.'

Alasdair shifted her more comfortably on his lap, his hold still firm enough to rid Kate of any ideas about struggling.

'I would be lying,' he told her, 'if I said I didn't want you. From where you're sitting it must be obvious.'

Colour rushed to the face he was smoothing against his shoulder.

'But don't worry,' he went on. 'I won't do anything about it. Unless you want me to.'

'I don't go in for this kind of thing,' she said flatly.

'Why not?'

'It's never worth it,' she said with a sigh.

Alasdair laughed softly. 'It can be, my sweet.'

'For you, maybe, but not for me.'

'So at this moment,' he went on, his tone so clinical he might have been discussing some experiment, 'despite the pleasure I'm taking in just holding you in my arms, your only instinct is escape?'

Kate wished it was. 'I won't say this is unpleasant,' she agreed, her tone matching his, 'but if I'd thought it was taken for granted as part of the day's entertainment I would have driven straight home after lunch.'

'So that's it.' Alasdair's chuckle vibrated against Kate's breasts. 'I've got it!'

'You've got what?'

'Why you're so prickly these day, Kate Dysart.' He smiled into her eyes. 'You loathe being taken for granted. Thinking back, I suppose I did it all the time up at Cambridge. Then I compounded my sins when I turned up in Foychurch like a bad penny, taking it for granted you'd drop everything to spend time with me. And now, as far as you're concerned, I'm doing it again.'

'True, as far as it goes,' she agreed. 'But it's not what bothers me most.'

'So tell me.'

'I'm suspicious about *why* you're doing this.' Kate eyed him narrowly. 'You never even saw me as a female in the old days, let alone someone you wanted to make love to. So why now all of a sudden? And please don't say you took one look at me outside school that day and the scales fell from your eyes, because I'm not stupid, Alasdair.'

'I've never thought so before,' he agreed, 'but for once in your life you can't work out the equation. It's simple. I'm a man, and you're a *very* desirable woman—'

'You mean you expect to take me to bed?'

'I want to. But that's something I'm *not* taking for granted. Right now I'll settle for just holding you like this for a while.'

Kate yielded as he clasped her closer, frowning as she thought this over. It was undeniably good to feel close to Alasdair like this. She liked the warmth and strength of him, and it was all just as she'd dreamed it would be, over and over again when she'd fantasised about it in the past. But in those days her fantasies had never gone as far as actually making love with Alasdair. Yet now, long after she'd given up dreaming, he wanted her. So maybe...

'What are you thinking?' he asked after a while, his touch so light Kate didn't know he'd removed the pins from her hair until it came tumbling down.

'I was thinking that if you did want to take me to bed perhaps it might be a good thing,' she said thoughtfully, and felt him tense against her.

'Would you say that again?' he demanded.

'I'm sure I don't have to.'

'So why do you think it would be a good thing? From my own point of view it's a ravishing idea, of course, but—'

'I think it would give me closure.'

'Closure?' Alasdair put an ungentle finger under her chin to raise her face to his. 'What the hell does that mean?'

Kate looked at him defiantly. 'Meeting you again has revived old ghosts. Maybe going to bed with you would lay them for good.'

Alasdair's eyes glittered like ice chips. 'Any time you go to bed with me, Katharine Dysart, you'll be too occupied to think of laying ghosts.'

'Ah. I've insulted you.'

'Damn right.' He took her by the elbows and planted her back in the other corner of the sofa. 'As an ardour-dampening exercise, that was very effective.'

Kate looked pointedly at his lap. 'Not entirely.'

He jumped up, and kicked some logs into place in the fire. 'All right,' he snapped, his rigid shoulders very expressive. 'I've changed my mind. Maybe you should go home right now.'

'You're throwing me out?'

Alasdair turned on her. 'I thought you were desperate to go?'

'Not at all. If you remember,' she reminded him, 'I was saying it might be a good thing if you made love to me.'

He glared at her. 'When a woman makes love with me I prefer it to be for the right reasons.'

'Panting with lust for your body, rather than engaged in an experiment?'

'Exactly. So if your only aim is research, Madame Curie, choose someone else. Your friend Jack, for instance.'

'You're missing the point,' she said impatiently. 'It has to be you.'

Alasdair stared at her in frowning silence for a while. 'Explain,' he said at last.

'Seeing you again made me wonder if you're the reason why I find close relationships with men so tricky.' She gazed up at him coaxingly. 'So perhaps if we did make love I could just get it out of my system and—'

'Stop right there,' he ordered, his face like thunder. 'Are you seriously asking me to make love to you to set your libido free for other men? What the hell do you think I am?'

'My friend? A close, valued friend?' She got up and

went to him, sliding her arms round his waist. 'You wanted me a few minutes ago,' she muttered into his chest, and moved closer, triumphant when she felt him harden against her. 'I think you still do.'

He gave a smothered exclamation and pushed her away. 'Stop it, Kate. If you want to play games find someone else.'

She turned away to hide sudden, unexpected tears. 'Alasdair, I'm sorry,' she said thickly. 'It was a stupid idea. If you'll get my coat I'll go home.'

He turned her round and found her eyes were wet. 'Kate—don't, please. Come and sit down again.' he drew her down beside him on the sofa and put his arm round her, frowning when she stiffened.

'Change of heart?' he asked, his cheek against her hair.

'No. Embarrassment,' she said gruffly.

'About what?'

'Suggesting something so idiotic.'

Alasdair was quiet for some time. At last he turned her face up to his. 'I know this is a long shot, but tell me the truth. If we did make love, Kate, would it be the first time for you? Is this why you're choosing me for the experiment?'

'No.'

'Then what's the problem?'

'Me. I'm the problem.'

'Tell me about it.' He ran caressing fingers through the long, silken strands of hair. 'Because if some idiot's said you're frigid—'

'Not frigid, exactly.' A quiver of laughter ran through her. 'But for your ears only, Alasdair, part of me sort of stands apart during the process, amazed I'm doing something so ridiculous.'

He grinned involuntarily, then sobered. 'And are you saying this is down to me?'

'In the most peripheral of ways, I suppose it is.' Kate removed herself from Alasdair's sheltering arm and sat in the corner of the sofa, facing him. She secured her hair back behind her ears, hesitated, then took in a deep breath.

'You really want to know what happened to me before you left Cambridge to take on the world?'

His eyes narrowed. 'You know damn well I do. So talk.'

She turned her head to stare into the fire. 'Once upon a time, as they say, you never even noticed that I was crazy about you, or if you did you never took it seriously.'

And for the best part of two years Kate had managed to live with her unrequited passion, trying to be content with the few odd hours she spent in Alasdair's company, firmly repelling all other male interest, and, unlike most of her peers, working too hard to leave much time for play. Then her world had fallen apart. The unthinkable had happened. Alasdair Drummond had acquired a woman in his life. And it had been obvious to Kate, and to everyone else in their vicinity, that the relationship had become sizzlingly physical from the moment Lisa Bryant moved into Alasdair's orbit.

'Lisa,' he said blankly. 'Good Lord, I'd forgotten about her.'

Kate sniffed. 'I wish I had. Her brother was on my course. She came to visit Jon one day, he took her to the pub, and you were there. With me. But you forgot I existed once the luscious Lisa arrived. Nor was yours the only tongue hanging out. But it was the only one she fancied.'

'She was quite a girl,' he said reminiscently. 'No brain, but a shape to tempt a saint.'

'And I hated her guts!'

Alasdair frowned. 'But it didn't mean anything. It was just a fling, Kate, for both of us.'

'Some fling. You spent most of it in bed, according to Jon.'

'But surely Lisa wasn't the reason you locked yourself away like that?'

'No. But from a scientific point of view she was the catalyst.' Kate sighed. 'And this is where it gets really pathetic. I had a brainwave. I decided it was time you woke up to the fact that I was a woman, too. So I set out to make you jealous.'

He stared, astonished. 'Who with?'

Her chin lifted. 'Since you never even noticed, his identity hardly matters.'

Alasdair's eyes hardened. 'What happened?'

'Once you were distracted by the luscious Lisa one of my more persistent followers moved in on me, so I seized my chance. He was a charmer—clever to. I liked him a lot. Otherwise,' she assured him, 'even to make you jealous I couldn't have done it.'

'Done what?' said Alasdair with foreboding.

'For the best part of a week, hoping you would notice and burn with jealousy, I led my Romeo on shamelessly.' Kate gave a bitter laugh. 'And the end result was disaster.'

Hardly able to believe his good fortune, the young man had armed himself with champagne when Kate invited him back to her room. And in sore need of Dutch courage Kate had let him fill her glass too often, so that when he'd begun to make love to her she'd been in too fuzzy a state to keep him at arm's length.

'In no time at all we were on my bed,' she went on. 'Odd the things one remembers. His hands were shaking, and he was sweating, and suddenly things really got out of hand.'

'He raped you?' said Alasdair through clenched teeth.

Kate looked at him consideringly. 'If you mean that I wasn't willing to go that far, then I suppose technically you could say he did. And because I wasn't—well— fired up for it in the way he was, it was a painful, humiliating experience that gave the poor lad no satisfaction at all.'

Alasdair glared at her, incensed. 'He raped you and you can call him a poor lad?'

'I led him on, remember. He had every right to think I was willing. And, to be fair, he had no idea it was my first time. Though ultimately he was left in no doubt.' She bit her lip, feeling her face grow hot. 'At the time it was quite ghastly for both of us, but looking back I can see the funny side of it now.'

'I fail to see the joke,' snapped Alasdair.

'It wasn't much of a joke at the time,' Kate admitted. 'Nor is it easy to describe. Politely, anyway. The thing is, Alasdair, I was never a sporty type, in school or out of it. So when my Romeo finally got to first base with me, he came up against a barrier other girls lose simply by playing ballgames or riding horses, if they even had much of one in the first place. Mine was very firmly in place, alas. And, no matter how much I resisted, my would-be lover, who was in quite a state by this time, was determined to succeed. By the time I felt something tear inside at last I was exhausted and hysterical, and it was all over for him in a flash. And when I shoved him away at last poor Romeo was utterly appalled.' Kate pulled a face, unable to look at Alasdair.

'*Why?*'

She drew a deep breath, and shrugged ruefully. 'I don't have to draw pictures, surely, Alasdair. Let's just say my virginity was proved beyond all possible doubt, to Romeo's horror. Mine, too.'

There was silence between them for a while.

'And that's why you locked yourself away?' Alasdair said at last.

She nodded. 'The only one who knew what happened was Romeo. I stayed immured in my room for the rest of term, other than lectures and exams. And the odd dash to the shops.'

He stared at her in disbelief. 'And you depended on this idiot never to tell anyone?'

Kate smiled crookedly. 'I told him that if he said he'd scored with me I'd broadcast every last gory detail.'

Alasdair swore under his breath. 'He must have kept his word, whoever he was, because I never had the least idea. I wish to God I had. I was hellish worried about you.'

'Is that why you contacted me so often after you left?'

'In some ways. But I would have done anyway.' His hand tightened on hers. 'I was very fond of you, Kate.'

Kate scowled. 'So why were you so utterly horrible to me when you came to Friars Wood that last time?'

'You'd changed out of all recognition. Instead of the sweet little kid I'd been so fond of I found a cold, hostile young stranger, nothing like the Kate I'd known before. I felt so guilty, sure that I was to blame in some way for the change. Which it seems I was, indirectly,' he added heavily.

'It wasn't your fault, Alasdair,' she assured him, 'only mine for being such a fool.'

'Adam said you were in Italy for most of that summer afterwards. Why did you stay away so long?'

She looked away. 'I thought you might have worked that one out already.'

Silence fell, and lengthened until the sudden crash of falling logs broke the spell. Alasdair got up to see to the fire, then turned to look down at her.

'You mean you were pregnant?' he said quietly.

'No.' She shrugged. 'In the circumstances the scientist in me knew that was highly unlikely. Which didn't stop me from feeling afraid I might be.'

'Didn't the idiot use protection?'

'Oh, yes.' Kate looked away. 'Unfortunately it—it wasn't equal to the occasion.'

Alasdair swore softly and sat down again to put his arm round her. 'Which must have resulted in weeks of purgatory for you.'

'Not that long, actually. Lorenzo, my sister's husband, called in his personal friend, Dr Bruno Tosti. Due to Bruno I knew straight away that I wasn't pregnant, and the blood tests he took proved that I was suffering from nothing else more terrifying than mild anaemia.' Kate leaned against him as she felt him relax. 'Jess insisted I stay with her until I felt better. So I spent the summer taking iron pills, eating good food, playing with my nephew and lying in the sun.'

'What happened when you got back to Cambridge? Did you meet up with Romeo again?'

'No. He was a year ahead of me, thank heavens, so he'd left by then, which made things easier in some ways.' She sighed. 'But life was hard in others because there were two things missing from it. You, for one. The other was my enthusiasm for research. Which, dear reader, is how I come to be teaching little darlings of both sexes in Foychurch.'

Alasdair pulled her closer. 'So now I know the whole story. Or is there more I should know?'

She twisted round to look up at him. 'You don't *have* to know anything about me, Alasdair Drummond. I wouldn't have embarked on my life story tonight if I hadn't had the silly idea of seducing you. I must remember not to do it again. It never turns out well for me.'

'As an experiment,' he reminded her sardonically. 'I've had more flattering offers.'

'I bet you have!' Kate looked at her watch and stood up. 'Time I was off. Which is a pity. This fire is too tempting to leave.'

'Do you have to leave?' he said, getting to his feet.

'Are you offering me the use of your spare room?'

'If you insist. But the bed's more comfortable in mine.' He smiled down at her. 'Not that I have a hope of persuading you to join me in it, of course.'

'You give up too easily,' she said rashly, and found herself yanked hard against Alasdair's chest.

'Fighting talk,' he muttered, and turned her face up to his.

This time, her emotions running high after her revelations, Kate's mouth responded so passionately to his that in seconds they were straining each other close until the inequality in their height threatened to overbalance them. With a smothered laugh Alasdair picked her up and sat down with her on the sofa again, still kissing her as he bore her back into the cushions. He slid his hands into her hair to look down into eyes which gleamed up at him, molten gold in the firelight.

'Do you know,' he said, in a tone that sent shivers

down her spine, 'what this seductive hair of yours does to me, Kate?'

She stretched against him deliberately. 'Do I have nothing else to recommend me, then?'

'Your eyes. Your mouth—' He backed up his statement with kisses, and went on kissing her until she was restless and breathless in his arms. 'And these,' he said hoarsely, as his hands slid up beneath her sweater. She clenched her teeth to stop them chattering as he released the catch which delivered her breasts naked into hands which cupped them so that he could kiss the satin-skinned slopes. Alasdair took such a long, savouring time over it that when his lips found her expectant nipples at last she gave a smothered gasp, and dug her nails into his back through his shirt. At the precise moment the exquisite torture became unbearable Alasdair moved his mouth back up hers, his tongue penetrating as he spread her hair out on the cushions. On fire from head to foot by this time, Kate thrust her hips against him, her body vibrating with need and anticipation against his.

'Do you mean it?' he demanded hoarsely.

She nodded mutely, and he got up, bent to put a guard in front of the fire, then turned back to pull her to her feet and lead her from the room.

To Kate it was an increasingly unreal experience to go hand in hand with Alasdair up into the darkness of the upper floor. So unreal that somewhere along the way she lost her urgency. She kept looking up at his tense profile to convince herself that this was really Alasdair, dream lover in the past, but now soon to be lover in fact. But when she stopped dead, in disbelief at the prospect, Alasdair picked her up and carried her the rest of the way. He sat down with her on his lap on the edge of the bed in his room, and Kate looked up at him, her eyes enormous in the semi-darkness.

'Changed your mind?' he whispered.

Feeling it was too late now, even if she had, Kate shook her head.

'Are you sure?' he said huskily.

'Oh, well, if you're going to argue about it—' She gave a smothered cry of protest as he tossed her onto the pillows and let himself down on top of her, taking her breath away.

'I never argue with a lady,' said Alasdair. And, giving her no time to recover, he undressed her with the speed and skill of someone familiar with the task, laughing indulgently when she turned her back as he stripped off his own clothes. Kate lay with her head buried in the pillow, no longer sure about this at all. This was Alasdair, she reminded herself. What if she disappointed him? It had happened before. Then she gasped as he flipped her round and held her against his naked, aroused body. At which point Kate discovered that her own body had turned into one great erogenous zone from head to foot. She shivered, and clutched at him with feverish hands, and Alasdair laid her flat and knelt over her, fighting for control.

'Wait,' he said breathlessly, and slid his hands into her hair to look down into her eyes. 'I want this to be as beautiful for you as I can make it, Kate. And different. So lie still, darling—at least for a while. Let me love you as you should be loved.'

Kate gave a deep sigh, and submitted herself to the bliss of the moment as he kissed her. It was a long time before his mouth left hers at last to make a slow, arousing journey downward to set her on fire again as his lips and fingertips caressed her sensitised, quivering nipples, sending streaks of fire down to the part of her which dissolved in anticipation as his mouth moved lower. She tensed, her breath tearing through her chest as his fingers probed to test her readiness, then her eyes opened wide as he found the hidden core of her response.

Kate gave a hoarse, disbelieving little cry as waves of sensation coursed through her and Alasdair held her close, murmuring such gratifying things in her ear she opened dazed, disbelieving eyes at last, straight into the molten gleam in his.

Quick to read her mind, he smiled in reassurance. 'It is me. And this is you. And it did happen. Keep looking at me, Kate.' and with one smooth, sure thrust he entered her and held her still.

Kate lay unmoving for long, breathless moments, gazing up at Alasdair as her body adjusted to the throbbing reality of their union. Then her eyes widened in surprise as she felt her innermost muscles clench round him in response. Instantly he thrust deeper, and kissed her open, gasping mouth, his hands threading through her hair as he began to move in her and with her, coaxing her body to answer his, his patience so absolute that at last Kate lost hers, and arched against him in imperious demand. He responded fiercely, the rhythm of their loving mounting as it grew wilder and faster until she cried his name in disbelief as she climaxed, and he crushed her close as he surrendered to his own release.

Almost at once Alasdair rolled over, taking her with him to hold her close in his arms, his cheek on her wildly dishevelled hair.

'This,' he whispered, pulling the covers over them, 'is where I ask ''how was it for you''?'

Kate thought it over, waiting until her breathing was normal enough for her to answer. 'Different,' she said at last, pushing her hair back from her eyes. 'So different that it's hard to believe it was the same basic process as the other times.'

'Times plural?' he said sharply, and reached out to switch on a lamp so he could see her face.

'Well, yes. It's a long time since the anonymous Romeo.'

Alasdair propped himself on an elbow to look down at her. 'So you'd already made one experiment. One that you're telling me about, anyway.'

'I didn't think of it as an experiment. I met Julian when I was doing my teacher training.'

'And?' prompted Alasdair coldly.

'For a whole term we got on very well. A fine romance, kind of thing. Not exactly no kisses, but certainly no bed.' Kate sighed. 'But when I got back to college after the Christmas break he asked me to marry him. When I said yes he required a more physical relationship.'

Alasdair drew her close, his lips against her cheek. 'Was it a repeat of the first time?'

She shook her head. 'It couldn't be in one way, obviously. And at least Julian seemed to enjoy it.'

'But you didn't.'

'Not much. It seemed only polite to try to fake it. But that didn't work. So by half-term the affair, if you could call it that, was over.' Kate sighed. 'Julian wasn't interested in being just friends. Which was a pity, because I was fond of him. And after that I decided sex was just too much trouble to bother with.'

Alasdair kissed her fleetingly. 'And how do you feel about it now?'

'Astonished.' Her colour rose as her eyes met his. 'As

I'm sure you could tell, there was no faking involved this time.'

He laughed, his eyes triumphant. 'I know. And now, my dear Miss Dysart, I'm going to prove it was no fluke.'

And to Kate's surprise and ultimate rapture Alasdair did as he said, taking so long over the process she was driven to pleading with him by the time he engulfed her in such an overwhelming cataclysm of pleasure that she fell asleep in his arms afterwards.

She woke to the touch of his caressing fingers in her hair.

'Darling,' he whispered. 'It's getting late, and its raining cats and dogs out there. Ring home and say you're staying the night.'

Kate shot upright, blinking and yawning as she looked at her watch. 'Eleven!' Conscious of her nudity, she scrambled out of bed in ungraceful haste. Alasdair watched with deep enjoyment. 'I must go,' she said, frantically searching for her clothes.

Alasdair slid to his feet and pulled on a dressing gown. 'You can't drive home in this. Besides, we have things to talk about.'

'But I *must* go—' she began, then frowned. 'What things?'

'What happens next,' he said, taking her by the shoulders.

Kate stared at him blankly. 'But I told you. I drive back to Foychurch tomorrow.'

'I know that,' he said impatiently. 'I'm talking about us, Kate. Where do we go from here?'

'I thought you were coming to see me next week.'

Alasdair gritted his teeth, and gestured towards the bed. 'Did you hear any of those things I said just now?'

Kate looked away, but he jerked her head back.

'To refresh your mind, Katharine Dysart, I said I loved you.'

Her eyes fell. 'I assumed that was just good bed manners.'

'You obviously have a lot to learn on the subject.' said Alasdair coldly. 'It happens to be something I've never said before.'

'Not even to the lady in New York?' she said tartly, forgetting she was naked.

His eye narrowed to slivers of steel. 'No. Nor to anyone else until tonight. So pay attention. I love you, Kate. In some ways I did even back then, at Cambridge. But now it's different. You're a woman, and I want you. I've no intention of losing you a second time.'

Kate looked at him in such unflattering disbelief Alasdair turned away.

'Since you're obviously not going to stay the night you'd better get dressed,' he flung over his shoulder.

Kate made some hasty repairs in the bathroom, pulled on her clothes, and borrowed Alasdair's brush to tame her hair, her mind working overtime. At last, when she could put off the moment no longer, she went down the stairs Alasdair had left brightly lit for her and found him in the kitchen, making coffee.

'If you're determined to drive home,' he said curtly, 'you'd better drink this first. And give your parents a ring before you start out so they don't worry.'

'I always do that,' she said defensively.

They sat at the kitchen table in tense silence, facing each other over steaming mugs of coffee.

'So,' Alasdair said at last. 'I rushed things, obviously.'

'And astonished me.' She eyed him uncertainly. 'Did you really mean what you said?'

His eyes kindled. 'It's hardly a joke! So perhaps you'd be kind enough to tell me how you feel about me.' He smiled mirthlessly. 'One thing you must admit, Kate. The experiment was a success. You wanted to know if sex could be something you enjoyed, and unless you're the best actress never to win an Oscar you did enjoy it. With me,' he added significantly.

'I did,' she said without hesitation. 'It was bliss, Alasdair. But I never expected you to bring love into it. I used to dream that you would once, of course. But the dreams stopped dead after my farcical bid to make you jealous.'

His face set into a blank mask. 'By which I take it my sentiments are not returned?'

'They are to some extent,' she admitted. 'I admire your intellect, I like and respect you, and physically you turn me on like no man has ever done before.' She braced herself. 'But I'm not in love with you any more, Alasdair.'

CHAPTER EIGHT

THE silence was so absolute in the room Kate was sure her gulping was audible as she drank her coffee. As a conversation-stopper, she though morosely, her last words had been a wild success. But she had meant every one of them. Her feelings towards Alasdair had changed long before meeting him again. She knew only too well that the embarrassing, painful incident which put paid to her famed virginity had been entirely her own fault. But, strive as she might to be rational, some errant part of her brain still held Alasdair to blame for it.

After a while Kate could bear the silence no longer, and got up. 'I must go.'

He rose to his feet, looming over her as he eyed her in a way which had little to do with the love he'd been declaring shortly before. He held out the jacket he had ready for her, and she slid her arms into the sleeves, wishing she had a magic wand to wave to get herself out of here and back home into bed right that minute.

Alasdair turned her round and zipped up her windbreaker, then smiled in a way that rang alarm bells in Kate's head. 'Despite our slight difference of opinion, darling, unlike your former lover, I shan't give up so easily.'

She frowned. 'You mean you're still happy to be my friend?'

He shook his head. 'Not happy, precisely, Kate. But I can be patient. I wouldn't be much of a scientist if I weren't.'

She sighed. 'It's such a pity the timing's wrong. If you'd told me you loved me years ago I'd have been in seventh heaven.'

'Then I'll just have to develop some miracle drug to revive your devotion,' he said lightly. 'Which night shall I come over to Foychurch?'

Kate's eyes widened. 'You mean you still want to do that?'

He smiled indulgently. 'You can't believe that what's happened between us tonight has put me off the idea, surely!'

'Oh. I see. You expect to make it a regular occurrence.' She looked at him levelly. 'What happened tonight was just what I meant it to be, Alasdair. An experiment. A wildly successful one, I grant you.'

'Thank you so much!'

'But,' she went on doggedly, 'it was also a one-off. I'm very grateful to you for proving—'

'Stop right there,' he ordered, his eyes glittering dangerously. 'All I've actually proved is that with me you can enjoy the act of love. But that's the point, Kate. With *me* and no one else.'

'You can't know that for sure.'

'I'm right. Believe it.'

Their eyes clashed for a moment, then Kate turned to take her cellphone from her bag. 'Time I was off,' she said brusquely, and dialled Friars Wood. After a brief conversation with her father, to give an idea of when she'd be home, she told him not to let her mother wait up, then turned to Alasdair. 'Goodnight,' she said awkwardly. 'Thank you for—for everything.'

'It was a pleasure.' he said, lips twitching, then took her by the shoulders and kissed her swiftly. 'Drive safely, and ring me the minute you get there. I'll be waiting.'

Kate nodded, and went with him to the front door. 'Don't come outside dressed like that.'

Alasdair eyed the sheeting rain with misgiving. 'I think you should stay.'

Kate wasn't happy about driving home through torrential rain herself, but she shook her head. 'I can't do that. I'm leaving home after lunch tomorrow.'

'Then for pity's sake go carefully.' He seized her by the shoulders and kissed her again. 'I'll see you Tuesday evening about seven.'

She nodded, then fled out into the rain, unlocked her car and dived inside, threw her bag in the back, and tossed the phone on the seat beside her. She backed round carefully, waved at Alasdair's tall shape silhouetted in the light from the hall, sounded her horn in farewell, then, with her windscreen wipers going full blast, drove out into the lane and started for home.

By the time Kate had skirted Gloucester and begun heading for Stavely she was heartily sorry she'd refused Alasdair's offer. There was a steady stream of traffic heading her way, among them heavy goods vehicles which covered her windscreen in spray which made driving conditions nerve-racking. Progress was slow. And she was tired. Making love with Alasdair was not only different from anything experienced before, it was also a great deal more exhausting. Right now she'd have given a lot to be tucked up with him in that huge bed of his. Just to sleep.

She drove on, keeping doggedly to the speed limits, and doing her best to keep out of trouble when she was forced to put on speed to overtake a slow-moving lorry or slow down to let an overtaking car slot in in front of her. Eventually the road narrowed to one-lane traffic, which made things marginally easier, with no choice other than to drive nose-to-tail with the vehicle in front. It seemed like hours before Kate, feeling utterly shattered by this time, swooped round a sharp curve and saw a familiar rise up ahead. Almost home.

As she moved down a gear to allow for the climb, her phone rang. A glance showed that it had slid to the floor at some stage, and, keeping her eyes straight ahead and one hand firmly on the wheel, Kate reached down for the phone as she topped the crest of the hill. There was a sudden blinding glare from approaching headlights and she dropped the phone, gasping as the car went into a skid when it met water pouring across the road. She hauled on the wheel, her feet hard on the pedals as she tried to right the car, but as the road dropped away on the other side of the hill she lost control. The car veered across the road, shot through a hedge, and Kate screamed as she was hurled into a whirling, somersaulting chaos which ended in sharp, agonising pain before the world went black.

Glad to wake from the nightmare, Kate lay very still, too exhausted even to open her eyes, but very grateful to find herself at home in bed. Terrible headache, though. She would take some painkillers when she got up. But not just yet. More sleep, she decided, and slid back into oblivion.

When she surfaced again she could hear a strange beeping sound. She was still horribly tired. Her eyelids seemed weighted down. The effort to open them was enormous, but she managed it at last. And wished she hadn't. She closed her eyes again, waited for a few moments, then opened them very slowly. But the unfamiliar room was still there. She was in a hospital. Trembling, she closed her eyes again. Not a nightmare after all, then.

'Kate,' said a voice. 'Wake up, Kate. Come on, I know you can hear me.'

She raised the heavy eyelids to see a nurse leaning over her, smiling in encouragement.

'Hello, at last. How do you feel?'

Kate tried to speak but her mouth was dry. 'Thirsty,' she croaked.

Propped up expertly to drink water through a glass straw, she tried to smile her thanks afterwards.

'You stirred a little an hour ago,' said the nurse, 'but you went back to sleep again. Just lie there quietly for a minute while I fetch Sister.'

Kate frowned. Then stopped frowning because it hurt. Now she had attention to spare for it she found her head hurt quite horribly, along with various other parts which hurt almost as much. She stirred, then lay still again when she found she was attached to a drip. And there were flowers in the room. Lots of them. How had they arrived so quickly?

The door opened and the nurse came in with a calm young woman in dark blue.

'I'm Sister Blackwell,' she announced. 'Well done, Miss Dysart. You're back with us at last. Tell me how you feel?'

Kate's lips moved in a ghost of a smile. 'As well— as can—be expected?'

'By which you mean sore and in pain, and totally disorientated,' said Sister, nodding. 'You were in a car accident, and you were brought here to Pennington General. You suffered concussion from a blow to the head. You lost a great deal of blood, which has now been replaced, but for the time being we shall keep you on a drip and attached to a monitor.'

Kate gazed at her blankly. 'How long?'

'That depends on your progress.'

'I meant—how long since I got here?'

'Three days ago. Your parents will return to see you later. In the meantime try to rest.'

When she was alone Kate lay very still, trying to assimilate the information she'd been given. Three days. Three days out of her life. But at least she still *had* her life. For which, by the sound of it, she should be grateful. And it was a good thing the nurse had called her by name when she woke up. Otherwise she wouldn't have the slightest idea what it was. She fought down a sudden rush of panic, reminding herself she'd been hit on the head. No wonder her memory was on the blink. But Kate's panic increased when the door opened and a total stranger came into the room.

'I have to be quick,' he said. 'Even a fiancé's only allowed a minute or two.'

Fiancé? Kate stared at him blankly.

He stooped to kiss her cheek, his eyes full of compassion. 'How are you?'

She tried to smile. 'I've been better.'

'Did you get my flowers?'

'I don't know. I've only just woken up.' She looked at the profusion of blooms on the window ledge. 'Are they over there?'

'Never mind that. Tell me what happened to you.'

'I don't know. They said I was in a car accident, but I can't remember.'

'Just as well, probably.' He took her hand very gently in his.

She looked at him in distress. 'You'd better know that

I can't remember you either. Not even your name. I wouldn't know my own if the nurse hadn't called me Kate.'

He smiled reassuringly. 'Don't worry. I answer to anything.' He turned sharply at the sound of voices outside. 'Look, I shouldn't be here. I just had to make sure you were all right so I sneaked in.' He leaned over to kiss her cheek again, and went quickly from the room.

When the door opened again a minute later Kate tensed, but this time it was the nurse.

'Right, then, Kate. Would you like another drink?'

Kate smiled gratefully, drank more water, then settled back against the pillows. 'My fiancé was just here,' she told the nurse.

'Again?' Nurse Dunn smiled with sympathy. 'Poor man. He's been haunting the place.'

Sudden tears ran down Kate's face. 'I didn't recognise him,' she said, so desolately the nurse took her hand and squeezed it.

'Don't worry. Your memory's just taking a rest, that's all. So don't try and force it. Try to sleep for a bit.'

When she was alone Kate lay very still against the pillows, trying to come to terms with her blank mind. In America they always asked you the name of the President, didn't they? She wondered how she remembered that, decided it was too much effort to think about, and went to sleep. When she opened her eyes again there were two people sitting beside her bed, a lady with grey curly hair and dark eyes, and a tall man with greying fair hair, both of them with identical expressions of painful anxiety.

Tears slid down Kate's face as they bent to kiss her. 'I can't remember anything.'

Frances Dysart gave her a careful hug and kissed her

cheek. 'Don't worry about that, Katharine Dysart. I'm your mother and this is your father, and we love you dearly whether you remember us or not.'

Tom bent to kiss his daughter, then cleared his throat noisily as he resumed his chair. 'Is your mind a total blank, darling?'

Kate sniffed inelegantly, but managed a smile, comforted by the fact that her response to them was instinctive and unmistakable. 'Afraid so.'

'The consultant says this is pretty standard procedure after a knock like yours,' her father assured her. 'Temporary memory loss. As you get better it should come back.'

'I've told them at school,' said Frances huskily, and blew her nose on a tissue.

'School?' Kate frowned. 'I'm a bit old for that, surely?'

'The school where you teach, darling,' said her father, clearing his throat.

Kate thought about it. 'Do I teach Physics?'

After a swift look at her husband Frances explained that Kate taught general subjects to eight-year-old pupils at Foychurch, a village in Herefordshire. 'A supply teacher's been called in while you're getting better.'

'Gabriel sent her love, and Adam will pop in again before he goes home tonight.' said Tom, then smiled at her blank look. 'Gabriel's married to Adam, your very worried brother, my darling.'

A subliminal flash of black curly hair and dark eyes swam into Kate's memory and out again. 'Adam,' she repeated, finding the name as familiar to her tongue as Mother and Dad had been.

Her parents went on to talk about Leonie, Jess and Fenny, and how all her sisters were desperate to see her the moment she was well enough, until Frances, aware that the new list of names was adding to Kate's distress, changed the subject to ask if there was anything she needed.

Kate smiled ruefully. 'A new memory would be nice.'

'Be patient, sweetheart,' said her father gruffly. 'Don't try to force it.'

'We'll come back this evening,' said Frances, looking at the exhaustion on her daughter's ashen face. 'By then you should feel stronger. I've brought clean clothes and various necessary bits and pieces. I'll let the nurse sort it out for you.'

When her parents had gone the nurse came in to check on Kate and see to her basic needs, then gave her a sponge down and a clean nightgown, and left her to have a rest.

'The consultant will be round later, Kate,' said the nurse cheerfully. 'My name's Michelle, by the way.'

Too late, when she was alone, Kate remembered she should have mentioned her fiancé's visit. She lay worrying about it. She had known at once she belonged to her parents. But there had been no similar response to the strange man. And surely, if she loved a man enough to become engaged to him, she ought to have felt some sense of relationship to him, too?

It was all too much, and, worn out by the sheer difficulty of life without a memory, Kate gave up and went to sleep.

Later she received a visit from the consultant, a genial no-nonsense man who came in with Sister in attendance to ask Kate questions about mental confusion, stiffness in her neck, and persistent headache or vomiting. She told him her lack of memory and sore, aching head were her main problems, apart from various cuts and bruises and the soreness in her chest. He told her the latter came from the restraining seat belt and would soon wear off, then assured her that the memory loss was likely to be fleeting.

'You were lucky, my dear,' he told her. 'You survived.'

Something Kate held on to with gratitude. To her surprise, when the nurse returned later to make enquiries about supper, Kate found she was rather hungry.

'So you should be,' said the cheerful Michelle, smiling. 'It's days since you ate anything.'

'I suppose it must be. I had steak and salad—' Kate stopped dead, her eyes enormous as she stared at the nurse. 'Odd that I can remember that, when everything else is blank.'

'It's a start! You'll soon have full recall, don't you worry.'

Kate knew the words sprang from a desire to comfort rather than medical expertise, but she smiled gratefully at the cheerful young nurse and agreed that some soup would be a good idea.

Once her patient had been fed, and given a drink and some mild medication for her aches and pains, Michelle bade Kate goodnight.

'I'm off now. Nurse Baker's taking over from me. See you in the morning.'

Kate lay very still, more tired from the simple task of eating and drinking than she would have believed possible. Not inclined to sleep any more, she thought about the school where she taught, and tried hard to bring it to mind. When it became obvious that this wasn't going to happen any time soon, she gave up and wondered how soon her aching head would let her read. When her parents came in she'd ask for some books. One thing she knew for certain, memory or not. She loved to read.

Even as the thought formulated there was a tap on the door, and a tall young man with curly black hair and dark eyes came in, brandishing a carrier bag.

'Hi,' he said, grinning. 'Sleeping Beauty's come back to us at last. And in case you're in any doubt I'm Adam.'

'I know,' said Kate, surprised. Because she did know. This, beyond any doubt, was her brother.

He bent to kiss her, a suspiciously bright look about the dark eyes as he straightened. 'Nice to have you back, half-pint.'

'Nice to be back.' She smiled at him valiantly. 'Even better when my memory gets back, too. Though where the family's concerned I don't seem to have too much problem.'

Adam took a radio cassette player from the bag, and with the air of a conjurer fished out several audio tapes. 'There. Gabriel thought you might not be able to read yet, so we bought you these to listen to instead. Jane Austen and Trollope, and a couple of thrillers just published—so even you can't have read them already.'

Kate gazed at them with such pleasure weak tears began to leak from the corners of her eyes.

'Hey,' said Adam in alarm. 'If you cry they'll throw me out.'

'I'm not crying. Pass me a tissue, please. And please thank Gabriel,' she added, blowing her nose.

'She's my wife, by the way,' he said helpfully.

'So I'm told,' Kate gave a strangled little laugh. 'This is mad, isn't it? One minute I'm driving along in a car, the next I wake up in here without a clue who I am— or who anyone else is either. Creepy!'

'But you did wake up, and you *are* here, Kate!

Nothing else matters. And now I must go, before they throw me out.' he added.

'They're very stingy with their visiting time here,' she protested.

'Making sure we don't wear you out.' Adam kissed her cheek and went to the door. 'Anything else you fancy, just shout.'

'How's the baby?' she asked, then gasped, her eyes locked with Adam's. 'I know you've got a baby!'

'Your godson Hal,' said her brother jubilantly. 'Henry Thomas on his birth certificate. And he's just fine.'

After he'd gone Kate had a little weep, but this time partly from thanksgiving. Memories were sifting through already, she comforted herself. After all, she'd only been conscious properly for a few hours. Tomorrow she might wake up and find her memory was in full working order.

A few minutes later the night nurse came in and introduced herself as Deborah Baker. 'But you can call me Debs,' she said, as she took Kate's temperature. 'You've got another visitor, and as it's your fiancé Sister said he could see you. But only for a little while. You've been out for the count for days, so we can't have you getting too tired your first day back with us.'

She opened the door and stood aside for a man to enter. 'Ten minutes,' she said firmly, and went out, closing the door behind her, unaware that she'd left her patient in a state of total shock. It was unlikely, thought Kate wildly, that she had two fiancés, even when she was in perfect health. Yet the man looking down at her was another stranger, totally different from the man who'd visited her that morning. Was she hallucinating?

'Hello, darling,' he said, when the silence threatened to stretch to the full ten minutes he was allowed. 'God, you gave me a fright, Kate. I thought you'd never come back to me.'

Kate stared at him in distress. 'I'm afraid my memory didn't turn up with me.'

He nodded. 'I know. I saw Adam on the way in.'

'Then you'll appreciate my problem.' She smiled apologetically. 'I don't even know your name.'

He stopped in his tracks, as though she'd dealt him a blow, and sat down abruptly in the chair Adam had left by the bed. 'In which case,' he said gruffly, 'it seems rather presumptuous to kiss you. I'm Alasdair. Alasdair Drummond.'

CHAPTER NINE

KATE studied the intelligent, handsome face, the brown curling hair and steel-bright grey eyes, and decided she liked the look of him, whoever he was. Alasdair, she thought, and nodded. 'At least the name sounds familiar, just like Adam's did.'

'Only I'm not your brother,' he said, his face relaxing slightly. 'In which case I think I deserve a kiss.'

To Kate's surprise he kissed her gently, but possessively, on her mouth, which responded a little, as though it knew his well. When he sat back, looking a little happier, he took her hand in his.

'Next time you come to my house, you stay the night,' he ordered. 'I don't want to have to go through that again.'

Kate smiled a little. 'Oddly enough, neither do I.'

He raised her hand to his lips, then held it tightly. 'I'll be later tomorrow because I'm going in to Healthshield for the day.'

'Healthshield?'

Alasdair's eyes flickered for an instant before he told her it was the name of the international pharmaceutical company he worked for. 'I've just returned from working for them in the States. Now I'm going to head up their UK operation. You don't remember, obviously?'

'No,' she said despondently, then gave him a troubled look. 'And it's not the only thing I can't remember. Alasdair, there was another man in here this morning. He said he was my fiancé, too.'

'*What?*' His eyes darkened ominously. 'Who in hell's name was it?'

'I haven't the slightest idea,' she said unhappily. 'I was hoping you might know.'

'What did he look like?'

Kate thought for a moment. 'Fairish hair, broad shoulders, and quite a bit older than you, I think.'

Alasdair's hand tightened on hers. 'Jack bloody Spencer, by the sound of it. And he got in here by saying he was your fiancé—?' He stopped short, and she looked at him questioningly.

'What's wrong?'

'Only a desire to punch Mr Spencer in the nose,' he said quickly. 'You belong to me, darling, and don't you forget it.'

'My memory's not very reliable at the moment,' she reminded him, and stared at him, puzzled. 'But why should this man say he's engaged to me?'

'Probably the only way he could get in to see you.'

'Is he a friend of mine?'

'An acquaintance,' said Alasdair curtly. 'Now, let's forget about him and concentrate on you. Has a doctor seen you today?'

'Yes.' Kate repeated what she could remember of the consultant's words, a process which tired her so much Alasdair got up, his eyes anxious.

'Darling, I must let you get some rest, or they won't let me come again.'

She tried to smile, but the effort was too great, and Alasdair bent to kiss her, this time on her cheek.

'It's possible I might not make it tomorrow, if I'm too late,' he said huskily, 'but I'll be here the next day, I promise, my darling. What shall I bring you?'

'Not flowers!'

He smiled as he glanced at the massed offerings on the far side of the room. 'Mine are among those somewhere. Shall I be boring and bring you grapes?'

'Just bring yourself.'

The grey eyes ignited. 'You mean that?'

Kate found she did. 'Yes.'

He bent and kissed her mouth. 'Much as I hate to leave you, I'd better go,' he said reluctantly. 'You just lie there and concentrate on getting better.'

'I'll do my best,' she promised.

After Alasdair had gone Kate was given a cup of tea, then tidied up and left to rest for half an hour before her parents arrived. When they did they looked slightly less anxious than on their first visit of the day, but this time they brought some get well cards, and read them to her, then arranged them on a shelf where she could see them.

'This is quite a big room. Is it costing a lot?' asked Kate suddenly.

Her father wagged a reproving finger. 'What does that matter, darling? You need peace and quiet for a while.'

'But when can I come home?' asked Kate, visited by a sudden wave of homesickness for the house overlooking the River Wye. Then felt another rush of astonishment and stared at her parents, hardly daring to breathe.

'What is it?' said her mother in alarm.

'I remember where we live!'

Grinning from ear to ear, her father took her hand and squeezed it, and told his wife there was nothing to cry about. 'You're doing splendidly, darling,' he told Kate.

'Sorry,' said Frances, sniffing valiantly. 'I haven't slept much lately. Which isn't surprising,' she added, with an indignant look at her husband. 'The bed's smaller than ours, and you take up a lot of room.'

'Are you in a hotel, then?' asked Kate.

'No, darling. Laura and Harry Brett are putting us up—Gabriel's parents. Which means we can pop in to see you more often. They've been so kind.'

'I need to know something,' Kate said abruptly, looking from one intent face to the other. 'Alasdair's been in.'

'We know, darling. He's been here a lot. He rang us late on Saturday night to see if you'd reached home.' Frances shivered. 'He was distraught when I said you hadn't. Then Chris Morgan came with the police to tell us what had happened to you.'

Tom took out a handkerchief and mopped his forehead. 'Worst moment of our lives.'

'I'm so sorry,' said Kate unsteadily.

'Alasdair said he wanted you to stay the night,' said Frances.

'I'd been with him?'

'Yes, darling,' said her mother, and smiled lovingly. 'We're so glad, by the way.'

'Glad?' repeated Kate.

'Alasdair got to the hospital before we did. He told us you got engaged that night.'

Tom smiled and patted Kate's hand. 'He asked our permission then and there, and although neither of you needs it we gave it gladly.'

Kate frowned and glanced at her left hand. 'If I had a ring I've lost it.'

'Alasdair hasn't had time to buy you one yet, Kate,' said her mother. 'Your headmaster, Mr Vincent, rang before we came, by the way. Told you to get better and not worry about anything. Though your little darlings miss you, he says.'

'That's nice,' said Kate. 'Who's Chris Morgan, by the way?'

'From the farm down below us. It was his fence you shot through. The car overturned as you careered down the bank into one of his fields,' said her father. 'Chris was outside with the dogs when it happened, so he rang the police and the rescue service on his mobile while he raced over to you. We owe him a lot.'

'What happened to the car?'

'Total write-off, but don't worry about that.' Tom patted her hand. 'We'll sort out another one when you're better.'

Kate groaned. 'I've caused such a load of trouble!'

'Why didn't you stay the night with Alasdair, darling?' asked Frances.

'I've no idea. I'll ask when I see him next.'

After a restless, uneasy night Kate was glad to see a friendly face when the nurse put her face round the door early next morning.

'Good morning. I'm to take you off the drip now, which will make life easier for you,' she was informed. 'Fancy a trip in there to the loo for a change?'

Giving fervent assent, once the drip had been removed from her arm, Kate was helped out of bed, wincing when every bruise on her body throbbed in warning as she shuffled painfully slowly into the adjoining bathroom. It was only after she'd washed her hands and brushed her teeth that she had the courage to face herself in the mirror. Then gave a gasp of horror which brought the nurse running.

'What is it?' she demanded, as Kate clung on to the washbasin for dear life.

'I've just seen the charming headgear, not to mention the face under it.'

'It's a bit bruised,' agreed the sympathetic Debs, and

put her arm round Kate to help her back to the bed she'd just made.

'A bit bruised!' said Kate, blinking back tears of self-pity as she slumped back against the pillows. 'I look like something from a horror film. This turban thing doesn't help.'

'You've got two lovely black eyes, it's true. But they'll fade. And at least you didn't break any teeth, or worse still your jaw.' Debs tucked in the sheets with practised ease. 'You could be looking like that man Jaws in the old James Bond film.'

Kate smiled weakly. 'Instead I bear a passing resemblance to Frankenstein's monster. Or maybe The Mummy?'

Debs laughed. 'Good to see you've got a sense of humour.'

'After seeing my face I need one!'

'How about the memory?'

Kate thought about it. 'Not too much success there, I'm afraid. Perhaps I'll get it back when my head stops aching. If it ever does.'

'I'll give you something for that after your breakfast. What would you like to eat? Full English?'

Kate shuddered. 'Just toast, please.'

After breakfast Kate felt better, able to adopt a more philosophical attitude towards her erring memory. It would come back, she told herself firmly, otherwise it wouldn't be giving her the odd flash of encouragement now and again. And her appearance would improve in time. She sighed despondently. It could hardly be worse.

After breakfast the nurse helped her to have a brief, sketchy bath, which tired Kate out but in other ways improved her well-being enormously.

'At least I don't smell any more,' she said, settling back against the pillows with relief.

'You didn't smell before!' objected Debs. 'I keep my patients in good nick, I assure you.'

'For which I'm very grateful.' Kate smiled at her, and won instant approval.

'That's better. I'm off now, until tonight. So you just have a good rest before Sister comes to see you.'

Kate was glad to do as she was told, and felt a lot better by the time Sister paid her a visit. Once the questions and answers were over Kate asked if she could listen to one of the audio books her brother had brought her, and after receiving permission lay listening while one of her favourite actors read the thriller Adam had found for her.

There were no more visits from strange men that day, but during the morning Frances Dysart came in alone for half an hour.

'Your father's tied up with an auction, but he'll come in with me this evening, darling. And tomorrow, if you're strong enough, Gabriel would like to visit.'

Kate smiled. 'Tell her to bring my nephew.'

Frances beamed. 'Adam said you'd remembered about his baby. He was over the moon.'

'So was I.' Kate bit her lip. 'Gabriel understands that I won't know her, does she?'

'Of course she does. Leo's coming down as soon as you're well enough—Fenny, too. And Jess is flying over soon.'

'Should she be doing that—?' Kate halted, her eyes suddenly bright. 'She's pregnant, isn't she?'

'Oh, yes, darling. She is.' Frances swallowed hard. 'There, you see? It won't be long before you remember everything.'

'I just hope I look less scary soon,' said Kate ruefully. 'I saw myself in the mirror for the first time this morning.'

Her mother nodded sympathetically. 'Your poor little face. But it's only bruises. By some miracle no bones were broken.'

'I was very lucky, wasn't I?' said Kate soberly.

After her mother left the day dragged for Kate. She couldn't concentrate on the taped story for very long at a time. Instead she found herself wondering how Alasdair was doing during his first day with his new workforce, and wished she could see him again to ask him. On the other hand, she thought, depressed, it was a miracle he was up for a repeat visit at all, the way she looked. Which brought her to wondering about her other surprise visitor. Looking back, she realised he'd never actually said he was her fiancé, just implied it. Probably he'd told someone that just to get in to see her. But why?

She found out when Adam came in to see her on his way home.

Once he'd asked after her, and settled on the chair beside her, he told her that a friend of hers had been in to the auction house.

'You remember that's where Dad and I work?' he asked.

'Only because Mother told me about it,' she admitted.

'It'll come.' He patted her hand consolingly. 'Anyway, the auction this morning was mainly furniture and silver, and a friend of yours made off with quite a few items. He asked me to give you his regards, and requested a visit when you were up for it. I said I'd pass on the message—'

'Are you talking about someone called Jack Spencer?'

Adam's eyes lit up. 'You remember him?'

'No, I don't. But he managed to get in to see me for a minute yesterday morning. I thought he said he was my fiancé, so imagine my surprise when a second fiancé, the real McCoy this time, turned up in the evening in the shape of Alasdair.' Kate pulled a face. 'He was furious when I described this Jack Spencer.'

'Spencer's niece is one of your pupils in Foychurch.' Adam gave her a quizzical grin. 'So what's all this about being engaged to Alasdair, then? Quick work when he's only been back from the States for a couple of weeks.'

Kate looked startled. 'Is that all? I've known him longer than that, surely!'

'You were up at Cambridge together. But that was years ago. You've hardly seen him since until now.'

'Odd. Because I was sure I knew him when he came in. Just as I did with you and the parents.'

Adam nodded slowly. 'It's not surprising. You were pretty close in the past. I suppose you just took up again where you left off.'

'I wish I knew,' she said in frustration. 'Did this Mr Spencer say when he wanted to come?'

'Whenever you like, apparently. It's something to do with his niece—Abby, he called her. Ring a bell?'

Kate sighed. 'No, it doesn't. But if he contacts you tell him to come if he wants.' She smiled at him. 'And please tell Gabriel I'm looking forward to seeing her. And the baby. And thank you for the tapes. They're a godsend.'

'Knew they would be,' said Adam smugly, and went home to his wife.

By the time Alasdair came to see her, bearing a basket of fruit and an armful of magazines, Kate had taken a lot more nourishment and rest, her headache was less intense, and he told her she was looking a lot better than when he'd seen her last.

'I could hardly look worse,' she said ruefully.

'Which doesn't stop me from wanting to get in there with you,' he informed her, after a kiss a shade too prolonged for the patient's pulse-rate.

'But I've seen myself in a mirror,' she said breathlessly, 'I could haunt a house.'

Alasdair grasped her hand tightly. 'Don't mention haunting. I never want to live through a night like that again.'

'But isn't that when we got engaged?' she asked artlessly.

His eyes flickered. 'That was earlier. You don't remember that part of the evening?'

'I don't remember anything much. Run it past me again.'

'You came to my house for tea, chose paint colours for the makeover I'm planning, then after dinner I took you to bed and made love to you,' he informed her, his eyes steady on hers. 'I did my best to make you stay the night, but you insisted on going home because you had to return to Foychurch and your job next day.'

'Bad move on my part,' said Kate ruefully.

'Very. Another time I'll command obedience.' His confident smile was so familiar she returned it involuntarily.

She knew that smile of old, she was sure. Yet she had a feeling that Alasdair was keeping something from her.

'By the way,' she said, 'Adam told me that my mysterious stranger, Jack Spencer, bought quite a lot at the auction today. He wants to visit me again.'

'No way,' snapped Alasdair. 'You hardly know the man.'

'It's something to do with his niece, Abby.'

'Not for the first time!'

'What do you mean?'

'That's how you met the man in the first place. You took the child home with you after school for a few hours until Spencer could collect her. Which doesn't give him the right to barge his way in here, pretending to be engaged to you.' Alasdair jumped up, apparently unable to sit still any longer, and Kate looked at him in surprise.

'Hey! Calm down. I want to know about your first day as head honcho.'

He turned back to her with a wry smile. 'Thought you'd never ask.'

After a full account of his first day as Operations Director at the UK arm of the global pharmaceutical giant, Alasdair looked down at her ruefully. 'I'm wearing you out.'

'No, you're not. I love hearing about it—'

'But you get tired easily, and I'm forgetting that.' he bent to kiss her cheek. 'I'd better go. But I'll be back tomorrow.'

'Thank you for the fruit.' She smiled at him. 'Such extravagance!'

'Not if you eat it all.' He frowned. 'I hope you are eating?'

'Yes, sir—of course, sir,' she said pertly, and Alasdair grinned and bent to kiss her mouth.

'Get well soon,' he said against her parted lips.

'I'm doing my best.'

'I don't doubt it,' he said huskily. 'Goodnight, darling.'

The following afternoon Kate received a visit from her mother, in company with an attractive young blonde woman who was easily identified as Gabriel, since she was carrying a baby.

'I came too, so I can whisk him out if he roars,' said Frances.

Gabriel eyed Kate's face with awe. 'Wow, Kate, what does the other fellow look like?'

'Actually, I'm improving,' said Kate dryly. 'You should have seen me a couple of days ago. Will I frighten the baby if I hold him?'

'Try it and see,' said Gabriel promptly, and handed her son over.

The baby lay quietly, looking up at Kate's bandaged head with such apparent interest the others chuckled.

'He's fascinated,' said Frances fondly.

'It comes off tomorrow. Perhaps he won't fancy me then.' Kate was gazing down at the baby so raptly she failed to notice the worried look exchanged by her two visitors.

'Does that mean you can come home afterwards?' asked Gabriel.

'I hope so.' Kate looked up with a smile. 'Everyone's marvellous to me here, but it's still a hospital. Some home cooking would be good. My appetite's coming back.'

'Wonderful,' said her mother thankfully. 'I'll go back home today, then, and get things ready. But I'm very grateful to your parents, Gabriel,' she added. 'They've been so kind.'

'Mother was only too pleased to help. She'd like to see you, too, Kate, when you're up to it.'

'Any time she likes, Gabriel—only tell her she'll have to introduce herself!'

Michelle popped her head round the door. 'There's a

gentleman here, Kate. Says he's a friend. A Mr Jack Spencer. He's got a little girl with him who's very anxious to see you, apparently. What shall I say?'

'You'd better tell him to bring the little girl in—say five minutes or so,' said Kate, surrendering her nephew to his mother.

'Don't let them stay long, darling,' said Frances. 'We'll be off now, but Dad will be in tonight, and probably Adam, too. So if there's nothing you need, I'll say goodbye until tomorrow.'

After they'd gone Michelle tidied the bed and gave Kate a drink. 'Ready for your next visitors? But they mustn't stay long, or Sister will have my head.'

'She could have mine with pleasure,' retorted Kate, and Michelle chuckled.

'You are getting better. Right, then. Lie still for a moment or two.'

She returned shortly afterwards to usher in the stranger Kate had already met. But this time he had a little fair-haired girl by the hand.

'Five minutes,' warned Nurse Dunn in official tones, and closed the door behind her.

'Hello, Kate,' said Jack Spencer, smiling. 'Abby wouldn't rest until she saw you herself, so I took her out of school for the afternoon and brought her along. Sister's permission to visit today, but I admit I resorted to false pretences the first time.'

'And confused me not a little,' said Kate with a smile, then turned to the child, who was regarding her with utter dismay. 'Hello, Abby. Don't be afraid. It's only bruises. I hurt my face in a car accident.'

The child swallowed hard, then, after prompting from her uncle, handed over an enormous get well card. 'From everyone in the class, Miss Dysart,' she said, in a wobbly little voice.

'How lovely!' Kate took out the card, her throat thickening as she saw the kisses and little drawings alongside a list of carefully written signatures.

'Abby was sure you'd been killed and we were keeping it from her,' said Jack, 'so I thought I'd show her you were very much alive, if not kicking. Now she can report back to her mates and tell them you'll soon be back with them.'

'Will you really, Miss Dysart?' said Abby, hope gleaming behind her glasses.

'Absolutely,' said Kate. 'But I need to get better first. Which may take a while. But as soon as I can I'll be back in Foychurch.'

'So tell your gang,' Jack Spencer instructed his niece, 'that they must work hard to show how well Miss Dysart's been teaching them. You included.'

'I will,' said Abby fervently, and, when her uncle nudged her, handed Kate a small package. 'This is from Mummy and Daddy.'

'Partly as a get well present,' said Jack Spencer, 'And partly for being so kind to Abby when the baby was born.'

Kate felt sudden panic. 'I'm afraid I don't remember—'

'Miss Dysart had a bad knock on her head, Abby,' he told his niece quickly. 'So she can't remember anything.'

'You took me home with you until Uncle Jack collected me,' said Abby.

'I'm glad I could help,' said Kate, feeling suddenly sick and hot as her head started to throb. The throbbing grew worse when she opened a jeweller's box to find a brooch with coloured jewels set like a delicate spray of flowers. 'How—how lovely,' she said faintly.

'Julia is very grateful to you. She would like you to have this as a token of appreciation,' said Jack, eyeing her uneasily. 'We'd better be off, Kate. Get well soon.'

CHAPTER TEN

AFTER Jack Spencer's visit Kate's escape from hospital was delayed by a respiratory infection which sent her temperature soaring.

'You've been prescribed a course of antibiotics,' said Sister. 'And,' she added firmly, 'not so many visitors, please, Kate. I shall inform your parents.'

Things grew hazy for Kate for a while after that. She was vaguely aware of being given medication and a drink and told to sleep, but the sleep was disturbed. Sometimes by her cough, at others by dreams—one of them so erotic she woke with a start, staring round her wildly, until her pulse subsided and she came to terms with the fact that she was in a hospital bed and not Alasdair's.

Alasdair! Her dream had been so vivid she could still feel the heat of his naked body against hers, his face buried in her hair as he brought her to such a state of frenzy she knew without doubt it had to be a memory instead of just a dream. But when her pulse slowed Kate's embarrassment gave way to triumph. Her memory must be coming back. At the thought her body relaxed, and this time when she fell asleep there were no dreams.

She woke fully at last to find her mother sitting beside the bed, her face pale and drawn as she held Kate's hand.

'Hello, darling,' she said thankfully. 'How do you feel?'

'Not wonderful. But better than last night.'

'I hope so, my darling,' said Frances gently. 'You were a little delirious for a while. But Sister told me your temperature's down today, and you should come on rapidly now.'

'Alasdair?' said Kate involuntarily.

'He came last night, but he was only allowed to see you for a minute. He's desperately worried, so I'll ring him and tell him you're back with us again.' Frances smiled. 'Are you up to seeing him tonight?'

'Of course I am.' Kate grasped her mother's hand tightly and smiled in reassurance. 'I feel much better. The pills must be working. How's Dad?'

'He's just having a word with Mr Murchison, darling. You know how your father is.'

'Likes every last detail, preferably from the man in charge,' agreed Kate, and smiled jubilantly. 'You see? My memory's on its way back!'

When Tom Dysart came in he beamed to see his daughter awake. 'That's better, sweetheart.'

After her parents had gone Kate decided to try a visit to the bathroom on her own, very pleased with herself when she managed it without mishap. She was even able to bear a look at herself in the mirror, pleased to find the puffiness had gone from her face and the bruises were fading. The turban-style dressing on her head was a bit of a turn-off, but on the whole, Kate decided, she looked a lot more like herself than the apparition she'd last confronted in the glass. When she was on her way back to the bed, as shaky on her legs as a newborn foal, the nurse came in and started scolding, telling her she should have rung the bell.

'Don't you get too cocky now, Kate,' warned Michelle. 'But since you are out of bed you may as well sit on that chair for a minute while I change your bed.'

'I'd like a bath,' said Kate firmly.

'Don't worry, I'll have you all fresh and lovely by the time your fiancé comes.'

'Fresh maybe,' said Kate, pulling a face. 'Otherwise I still won't win any beauty contests. Not,' she added honestly, 'that I would normally. But I promise I can look better than this.'

Newly bathed, sitting up in a freshly changed bed, wearing a clean nightgown and fragrant with her own perfume instead of antiseptic, Kate enjoyed her light supper. She was told afterwards that her brother had rung to ask after her and say he was away treasure-hunting but would be in tomorrow.

'A bit of a charmer, your brother,' said Michelle, reporting.

'He is. But spoken for, I'm afraid.'

'Always the way,' sighed the nurse, and handed over pills to swallow. 'Right. I'm off soon. Is there anything you need before I go?'

'No. I'll just lie here and concentrate on getting better.'

Kate lay utterly relaxed when she was alone. Because her parents had looked so tired and strained she had forbidden them to come back again a second time. So now all she had to do was wait for Alasdair.

Her wait was short. Barely ten minutes had passed before the night nurse popped her head round the door.

'If you're expecting someone tall, dark and gorgeous,' Debs whispered, 'he's here, champing at the bit. Do go in, sir,' she added aloud, in her best hospital manner. 'But not too long, please.'

Alasdair came in swiftly, his eyes dark-ringed in his haggard face.

'Darling,' he said huskily, and bent to kiss her cheek,

but Kate deliberately turned her mouth up, and with a stifled sound he covered her lips with his.

'You could give me a careful hug, too,' she told him, when he raised his head, and with an unsteady laugh he put his arms around her, but so gingerly she giggled. 'I won't break.'

'When you look as though you won't break in half I'll do better,' he promised. He released her carefully, sat down on the chair pulled up to the bed and took her hand. 'I came last night, but you were out of it so they wouldn't let me stay. You frightened the wits out of me. Again.'

'Sorry about that.' Kate's fingers tightened on his, and his eyes lit with a warmth which brought back her dream so vividly her breath caught.

'You remember me properly now, don't you?' he said triumphantly.

'Yes, I do, I'm beginning to remember a lot of things.'

'Among them the evening we spent before you insisted on driving off into the rain?'

Kate nodded. 'I thought the lovemaking part was a dream, but—'

'But what?'

'It was so real I knew it couldn't be.'

Alasdair kissed her hand, then turned it over and pressed his lips into her palm. 'The moment you're well enough I'll show you it was no dream, but a wonderful, mind-blowing reality, I promise.'

She smiled into his eyes. 'You'll send my temperature up again.'

To her surprise Alasdair's face hardened. 'It was Jack Spencer who did that.'

Kate frowned. 'How could he possibly be responsible

for a cough and a chest infection? It was just coincidence that it started after he brought his niece here.'

'All I know, Katharine Dysart, is that the man spells trouble,' said Alasdair grimly. 'I suppose he brought the entire contents of the local florist?'

'No, he didn't. Abby, his niece, brought that huge card over there, from my class. But Jack brought a present from Abby's parents. I can't remember what I did to deserve it, though.'

'You looked after the child at your place for a few hours,' said Alasdair shortly.

'That's what Abby said. No big deal, certainly,' said Kate, frowning. 'Would you get something from my locker, please? There's a small box in the drawer.'

Alasdair fetched it for her. 'Is this the present?'

Kate nodded. 'It's costume jewellery, but much too expensive for doing so little.' She took out the small, delicate brooch, and held the coloured stones up to the light. 'Pretty, isn't it?'

Alasdair stared at it malevolently. 'Costume jewellery?' he repeated, a note in his voice which brought Kate's head up in surprise. 'You obviously don't possess the Dysart eye, Kate. This is the Cartier piece Adam mentioned. He said Spencer fancied the thing. It was expected to fetch three thousand at auction.'

Kate dropped the brooch like a hot cake. 'You're not serious!'

'I am.' Alasdair rescued the brooch and thrust it back into its box. 'Whoever it's supposed to be from, I'd bet my last penny it was Spencer who paid for it.' He glared at her. 'Send it back.'

Kate bristled. 'Don't you dare order me about, Alasdair Drummond. I'm not eighteen any more.'

'Ah,' he said with satisfaction. 'So you remember back that far, then.'

'Not exactly. But I know we go back a long way.'

'Long enough for me to object to expensive gifts showered on you by other men,' he assured her tightly.

Kate thought of something. 'Do you know what Jack Spencer does for a living?'

'You told me he's some sort of builder—one with expensive tastes, obviously.' Alasdair sat down. 'If you'll give the brooch to me *I'll* send it back.'

'Are you always this dictatorial?' she demanded.

'Only where my woman is concerned,' he retorted.

'Your woman,' she repeated, eyeing him askance. 'Sounds a bit basic.'

He smiled crookedly. 'Where you're concerned, I feel basic. You belong to me, Kate, and don't forget it.' His smile deepened. 'Now, tell me about this dream.'

Kate shifted restlessly. 'We were making love. You were running your hands through my hair—'

'That figures. That wonderful hair of yours does amazing things to my libido, darling.' He leaned over and kissed her gently, then with increased heat when her lips opened to him. When he raised his head she smiled up at him radiantly.

'You're very good for me, Alasdair Drummond.'

'How?'

'I've seen myself in the mirror, remember? It's amazing you should want to come near me, let alone kiss me.'

His eyes blazed with sudden anger. 'I love *you*, Katharine Dysart. Bruised, battered, or all in one small, ravishing piece, it makes no difference. Remember that.'

'I will,' she whispered, her eyes brilliant.

'If you look at me like that I'll come in there and join you,' he growled.

'Promises, promises!'

He laughed. 'So when are you likely to get out of here?'

'Tomorrow this contraption comes off my head and I finish my pills, and if I'm very, very good I go home the day after, according to Sister.' Kate smiled at him. 'So depend on it—I'll be very good indeed.'

Next morning Kate woke with the feeling that something momentous was in store for her. Removal of the dressing, and maybe a shampoo to follow, she thought happily, and smiled as the nurse came in with her cup of tea.

'Morning, Debs. How are you?'

'I'm fine. And so are you, by the sound of it. These are the last of your pills, so down with them. Tomorrow you could be going home.'

'Which is why I'm chirpy!'

Kate ate breakfast, bade Debs goodbye until evening, and sat waiting in a state of great anticipation until Sister arrived, followed by Michelle with a dressing tray.

'Good morning, Kate,' said Sister cheerfully. 'Time to say goodbye to your stitches.'

Kate sat very still while the turban and the dressings underneath were removed. And registered something wrong. Horribly wrong.

'Your main problem was the blow to your forehead,' Sister informed her. 'It caused the bruising and swelling to your face, and contributed to the blood loss, but by some miracle your nose remained intact. There was another deep cut, high up on the back of your neck, probably due to broken glass, and I'm afraid your hair was so matted with blood and glass splinters it had to be sheared off to get at the wound.'

Kate sat in silence, not even registering physical pain as stitches were removed. She felt totally numb. Her hair had been her one great vanity, with never more than an inch at a time trimmed from it since she was a child.

When the session was over, Kate felt oddly light about the head. 'I'd like to go to the bathroom please,' she said politely.

'Wait for her, Nurse,' said Sister, then gave Kate an encouraging smile. 'Don't worry. You'll soon be back to normal.'

'Thank you, Sister.'

Alone behind the closed bathroom door, Kate leaned against it for a moment. Taking her courage in both hands, she went to the sink, stared down into it for a moment, then faced herself in the mirror. After one horrified look she felt the room swim round her, and she backed away to sit on the edge of the bath, her sore, shorn head in her hands. Stop it, she ordered herself fiercely. Otherwise they'll put you back to bed and keep you there until you can look at yourself without passing out. But all she could think about was Alasdair. Alasdair who found her hair so irresistible.

The dream came back in full force. Only this time it was recall, pure and simple. Shaking inside, she found she could remember their day together in every detail. Choosing colours for his walls. Eating dinner. Going to bed. Making wonderful, magical love together. A good thing she remembered it so well, she thought bitterly. Now she lacked the flowing hair which made Alasdair so hot for her he was unlikely to want a repeat performance.

Straightening, she stood at the basin again and examined her face, which was much improved. There was a light dressing on the scar on her forehead, and the bruises were fading rapidly. But the emergency haircut had left her looking like Peter Pan on a bad hair day.

'Kate?' Michelle tapped on the door. 'Are you all right?'

Kate opened the door, doing her best to smile. 'Not really.'

'What's wrong?'

'My hair. Or sudden lack of it.'

'It was long before the accident?' said the girl with sympathy.

'Silly at my age, I suppose, but, yes, it was.' Kate's mouth twisted. 'My one great vanity.'

'Hair soon grows. And they managed to treat your wounds without shaving it off, at least! The minute you're better you can have it trimmed professionally and you'll look great.'

Kate spent the day sitting in a chair, half hidden by the curtain at the window. At first her instinct had been to dive into bed and hide there. Instead she spent long hours staring, unseeing, at the rooftops of Pennington while she grappled with total recall of the past, and then went on to some hard thinking about the future.

After the lunch Kate didn't want she decided it was time to get dressed properly.

'No more lolling about in a dressing gown,' she told Michelle.

'I'll give you a hand.'

Kate was glad of it. By the time she was in jeans and jersey she was tired out.

'How feeble can you get!' she said scornfully.

'You're doing much better than anyone expected,'

said Michelle firmly. 'Now, you sit back in the chair and listen to your story, or whatever. And drink some of that water before I bring tea. You need plenty of fluids.'

Kate grew gradually more tense as the day wore on. When her parents arrived during the afternoon they did their best to hide their reaction to her hair with exclamations of pleasure that she was up and dressed and minus the turban.

'You look really cute with short hair,' said her father valiantly.

'Good try, Dad,' mocked Kate.

Frances gave her a disapproving frown. 'Your hair will grow again, Katharine. Just be thankful the rest of you survived.'

Katharine! Used in full only when her mother was cross with her. 'I know, I know,' said Kate wearily. 'It was just the shock. Seeing myself for the first time. I'll get used to it. Eventually.'

'You look very tired still,' said Frances, sighing. 'I'll be glad to get you home tomorrow and put you to bed in your own room.'

'I don't want to stay up there on my own, Mother,' protested Kate. 'I want to be downstairs with you, and go out with Pan and breathe some fresh air.'

'You remember Pan, then?' said Tom, beaming.

'I was wallowing so much in self-pity I forgot to tell you,' said Kate in remorse. 'I can remember pretty much everything now.' She reached in her pocket for the jewellery box and took out the brooch. 'How much did this fetch, Dad?'

'Good Lord,' he said, surprised. 'Where did you get that?'

'Mr Spencer brought it the other day, just as Mother was leaving. A present from his sister, he said.'

Frances gazed at the brooch incredulously. 'But that's—'

'Cartier,' agreed Kate. 'I hadn't a clue. I thought it was costume jewellery until Alasdair put me right.'

'You're not going to keep it, darling?'

'No fear. So come clean, Dad? What did you get for it?'

'Two thousand eight hundred,' said her father, bringing an exclamation of distress from his wife.

'Exactly, Mother,' sighed Kate. 'It's too much to accept, whoever gave it to me. And Alasdair's convinced Jack Spencer was just pretending it came from his sister so he could give me an expensive present.'

'But why would he do that?'

'Who knows?' said Kate, shrugging. 'Alasdair's convinced he's after my body. Which is a laugh. What man in his right mind would fancy someone who looks the way I do now?'

'You're feeling sorry for yourself again,' said Frances severely. 'And you're tired. So we'll go now, because Adam's popping in later. And no doubt Alasdair will be here this evening?'

'Yes.' Though she was dreading it.

'Then get some rest. I'll be back to collect you tomorrow, after you've seen the consultant, so please try to keep in one piece until I can take you home!'

Kate got back on the bed, glad to lie down for a while before supper. But she was back in the chair, lipsticked and perfumed, by the time Adam came in.

'Hi, half-pint,' he said grinning. 'Wow—great hair! The naughty schoolboy look. Mega-sexy.'

Kate laughed, despite herself. 'You sure do know how to make a girl feel good, Adam Dysart.'

'I get few complaints,' he said smugly, and perched

on the window ledge. 'So when are they letting you out of here?'

'Tomorrow, if I'm good.' Kate looked at him steadily. 'Seriously, Adam, do I look a fright?'

'Just because you've got short hair?' he said with scorn. 'Remember the time Jess had hers hacked off for Leo's wedding? It didn't put Lorenzo off much, did it?'

'True. But it's not Lorenzo I'm worried about.'

'You don't have to worry about Alasdair either.'

Kate wasn't so sure. By the time Alasdair arrived that night, later than expected, she was in a state of nerves which would have won Sister's deep disapproval.

When Alasdair came in at last he sucked in a breath as he saw the empty bed, then Kate said his name and he spun round, his relief so intense she relaxed a little as he strode across the room.

'You keep frightening the hell out of me,' he said fiercely, and bent to kiss her.

'Hi,' she said, her heart taking a nosedive when she saw the shock in his eyes as he straightened.

'Your turban's gone,' he said, after a pause which lasted a heartbeat too long.

'And most of my hair along with it,' she said flippantly. 'It's the latest thing. Peter Pan, wired.'

'Why was it cut off?'

'I've got a gash on the back of my neck. They couldn't get at it so they cut my hair off. With a blunt instrument, by the look of it. When I can I'll get it trimmed, but in the meantime—'

'In the meantime you can thank your lucky stars you survived,' he said forcibly, and clenched his teeth on a shiver. 'When I think of what could have happened I get nightmares.'

'I hope I don't.' She smiled a little. 'By the way, my

memory's resumed normal service. One look at the new me in the mirror this morning and that was it. Total recall'

He shot a look at her. 'So you remember what happened between us that night?'

'Yes, I do.' Kate held his eyes relentlessly. 'Also something that didn't happen. Which is all to the good, Alasdair. Because deep down you really can't cope with my new look, can you?'

CHAPTER ELEVEN

'THAT'S not true,' Alasdair retorted, but Kate shook her head in reproof.

'You're lying. Very gallantly, but lying just the same. Just as you've done ever since I got here,' she added. 'As I said, I remember every detail of our evening now—the meal, the lovemaking, most of the drive home, even—but one piece of the puzzle is missing. We didn't get engaged.'

Alasdair's face set. 'No, we didn't. But the only way I could get in to see you here at first was by saying I was your fiancé. Your parents heard about it before I could explain, and afterwards they were so kind to me about it I hadn't the heart to say it was a mistake.'

'Don't worry,' Kate said kindly. 'I'll tell them for you.'

'You don't have to.' Alasdair produced a box from his pocket and snapped it open. 'I've bought you a ring.'

Kate stared blankly at the large solitaire diamond.

'Try it on,' he ordered.

'No way,' she said flatly. 'I may be the one with the dodgy memory, but it's you who's forgetting something. I'm supposed to say yes, Alasdair, before you buy me a ring. Not only that,' she added, 'I'm sure that part of the reason you're doing this is because Jack Spencer bought me the famous brooch.'

Alasdair's eyes narrowed to chips of ice. He flipped the box shut and thrust it in his pocket. 'You're entitled to think what you please. But I bought the ring in good faith, Kate, because I thought we had something good together. Our minds have been in tune from the beginning. Intellectually we have a lot more in common than most people, plus blazingly good sex. People get married with a lot less reason to succeed than that—'

'Wait a minute,' she interrupted. 'Marriage?'

'It usually follows on from getting engaged,' he said, the hint of Scots very pronounced. 'But in the circumstances I can only apologise for taking too much for granted. Again.'

Kate looked at him thoughtfully. 'You know. Alasdair, I'm pretty certain that if I'd still been full of the old slavering puppy love when we met up again none of this would ever have happened. But straight on top of your rejection by what's-her-name—'

'Amy.'

'Right. Amy. She gave your ego the first knock, then it took another when my welcome was a bit lukewarm.'

'It was hot enough—eventually—when I took you to bed,' he reminded her angrily.

'No doubt about it,' she agreed. 'I had no idea sex could be like that.'

His face set. 'I thought we were making love.'

'Whatever it was, it was wonderful, Alasdair.' She smiled sadly. 'Strange, really. Even when my memory was on the blink I knew you were connected to me in some way the moment you came through the door. I couldn't put a name to your face, but even though everyone else knew you were my fiancé I couldn't quite believe it. I wanted to. I liked being engaged to you—'

'Then why the hell,' he said with sudden violence, 'won't you accept my ring?'

'The same reason as before, Alasdair. I'm not in love with you any more.'

He sprang up to lean over her, imprisoning her with his hands on the arms of the chair either side of her. 'I could make you love me—'

'You can't make people fall in love with you,' She smiled bleakly. 'I tried that myself, remember? It doesn't work.'

'Are you telling me you feel nothing at all for me?' he demanded.

'Of course not. I like you enormously, and physically you're the only man I've ever responded to—'

'But you can't face commitment to me?'

'No, Alasdair, I can't. Nor,' she added, 'will your life be ruined because I've turned you down. Will you please move away? You're crowding me.'

He straightened, every line of his body stiff with offence, and turned away to stare blindly through the window. 'So what happens now?'

'We let people know we're not engaged after all.'

'And what reason do we give?' He breathed in deeply. 'I know exactly what everyone will assume.'

'What do you mean?'

Alasdair turned, his eyes boring into hers. 'Think, Kate. Use that under-extended brainpower of yours for a change.'

She stared at him resentfully, then enlightenment dawned. 'Oh, I see. They'll think that you took one look at the new, unappealing me and ran for your life. Though why you hadn't done so already, when I looked far worse, will be a bit hard to explain.' She shrugged. 'We'll have to think of something else. Nothing for it— I'll just have to jilt you.'

'And who's going to believe that?' he said scornfully.

'My, my, put your ego away.' she mocked, then

looked down at her clasped hands. 'There is a reason I could give. But you may not like it.'

'I don't like any of this,' he said heavily. 'But go on.'

'My memory is doing reasonably well, but I remember nothing about the crash. Only what happened before it. My phone rang. Was it you?'

Alasdair was suddenly very still. 'I did ring you, yes,' he said tonelessly. 'Time was getting on, and I was anxious. It was such a filthy night I wanted to know you'd arrived home safely. It was around midnight.'

'I thought so.' she said, almost inaudibly, then raised her head to look at him. 'The phone had fallen on the floor of the car. When I reached for it I lost control of the wheel. That's the last thing I remember.'

He stood very still, his eyes locked with hers. 'So I'm to blame,' he said at last.

She shook her head. 'No, you're not, Alasdair. It was an accident.'

His mouth twisted. 'But if I hadn't rung at the wrong moment it wouldn't have happened.'

'No one else knows that. But if you prefer me to use that as a reason for ending our fictitious engagement I can. I can be mean and horrible and say I can't forgive you for it.' She smiled at him. 'Though until I saw your reaction to my hair I was going to suggest a passionate relationship of some kind, since we're so compatible in bed.'

He stared at her in disbelief. 'You mean the occasional session in the sack whenever your free time coincides with mine? Thank you so much. I've never proposed marriage to anyone before—'

'You haven't now,' Kate pointed out.

Alasdair paused. 'A mistake I'll rectify right now. Will you marry me, Katharine Dysart?'

'Thank you for asking, but no, Alasdair Drummond, I won't.' She smiled crookedly. 'If ever I do have a husband I'd prefer someone who didn't go pale at the sight of me.'

'That was just shock! It won't happen again.'

'No,' agreed Kate. 'It won't. I'm going home tomorrow, so you don't have to visit me any more.'

Alasdair's hands clenched into fists. 'I didn't *have* to visit you any other time. Can't you get it through your head that I was out of my mind with anxiety, Kate?'

'I know you were. Because you suspected you were to blame.' She patted one of his fists. 'Well, you don't have to worry about it any more. I'll soon be fighting fit, and back in Foychurch with my little darlings.'

'A prospect infinitely preferable to marriage with me,' said Alasdair bitterly.

'How successful could it possibly be? You seething with guilt over the accident, and me minus my one great attraction for you?' Kate shrugged. 'I vote I just tell everyone I've changed my mind. Lord knows you've been attentive enough since the accident, so no one will blame you for a moment, Alasdair. My family will be disappointed, but not surprised, I promise you.'

'Because it's happened before?'

'Exactly.'

Alasdair stared at her. 'I can't believe this,' he said flatly. 'I came here tonight with the ring, thinking you'd be pleased, fool that I am. I should have remembered.'

'Remembered what?'

'That you bear no resemblance to the girl I knew in the past.'

'True.' Kate sighed regretfully. 'She would have been ecstatic, poor innocent child.'

'But of course you've grown up since then,' he

mocked, then turned away when a knock on the door heralded an appearance from Nurse Baker.

'Time up, I'm afraid. Five minutes, then I'll be back.'

Alasdair turned back to Kate, his eyes wintry. 'So that's it. I can now get on with my life, free of all encumbrances, Miss Dysart.' He took her hand, smoothing a finger over the back of it. 'Is that what you really want?'

For a moment Kate almost wavered. Then she remembered the look on his face earlier. 'Yes,' she said firmly, 'it is. Good luck, Alasdair.'

He bent swiftly and kissed her hard on the mouth, then strode from the room, colliding with the nurse in the doorway as he went.

'Oh, dear,' said Debs, closing the door behind her. 'Lovers' tiff?'

Kate went home next day, but almost straight to bed, much to her disappointment. After the interlude with Alasdair she had spent a sleepless night that left her so exhausted she'd had to put on the greatest performance of her life to persuade the consultant that she was fit to go home. And when he had told Frances Dysart he was allowing this solely on condition that the patient was kept in bed for a couple of days Kate had resigned herself to her fate. Something it wasn't difficult to do when the greeting from Pan had knocked her flat before Tom Dysart could restrain him.

There had been pandemonium for a moment, then Tom had carried his daughter into the study and settled her on the sofa to recover.

'Now,' said her mother militantly, 'you see why you need rest. I'll give you some tea while you take a breather, then your father can carry you upstairs.'

'No way,' said Kate, horrified. 'I'll get up there under my own steam.'

'When's Alasdair coming to see you?' asked Tom.

Kate braced herself. 'I'm afraid he isn't. You may as well know right away. We're not engaged any more.' Not that they ever had been. 'I called it off.'

'Katharine!' said her mother despairingly. 'Why?'

'I don't *want* to get married.'

'Not even to Alasdair?'

'No.'

'Even though you've been in love with him all these years?'

Kate smiled sadly. 'That's the point. I fell out of love with Alasdair a long time ago.'

Tom Dysart, who had been listening in utter bewilderment, shook his head in deep regret. 'I don't understand. I like Alasdair. And he thinks the world of you, Kate. He was totally frantic when he arrived at the hospital that night, I can tell you. He rang us in a hell of a state when he couldn't get you on your cellphone.'

'I'd switched it off,' lied Kate, and closed her eyes wearily.

'Take the dog out for a walk, Tom,' ordered his wife. 'I'll make some tea, then off you go to bed, my girl, or I'll have to cancel next weekend.'

'What's happening then?' said Kate in alarm.

'Leo and Jonah are coming to see you. Fenny, too. I've put Jess off for a while, because I thought too many at once would be bad for you. And she's still at the morning sickness stage anyway, so Lorenzo will bring her when she's past the first trimester.'

Despite her protests Kate hadn't been at all sorry to be put to bed in her own room. With books to read, books on tape, her own television, and the familiar panoramic view of the river from her French window, it was a very pleasant place to convalesce. And later in the afternoon Gabriel brought the baby in to kick on a blanket on the carpet while they chatted, and to Kate's relief never said a word about Alasdair. Her brother, however, was not so restrained.

'You've given Alasdair the push,' he accused that evening.

'That's right.'

'Why?'

'Adam, I don't have to tell you why.'

'No, of course you don't,' he agreed swiftly. 'But I'm sorry, Kate. I like him.'

'So does everyone else.'

'Except you.'

'Wrong. I like Alasdair very much.'

'But he wanted a lot more than that, I suppose. Who could blame him?' Adam brushed a careful hand over her ragged crop. 'You look a bit tired, half-pint. I'd better leave you in peace and go bath my son.'

Resigned to the fact that she had no hope of returning to Foychurch before Easter, Kate settled down to the task of getting fit. She ate the nourishing food her mother fed her, and obediently kept to her room for a while, quite glad to do so when her visitors arrived. They were allowed into her room only on short visits, which Kate could handle a lot better than trying to cope downstairs where she was at everyone's mercy. Although warned in advance about her appearance, Leonie and Fenny were obviously shocked rigid at the sight of her, but to Kate's infinite gratitude Jonah gave her a hug and a kiss and told her she looked like a sexy little elf.

'It's such a shame you had to lose your beautiful hair,'

said Leonie, her dark eyes wet. 'When it grows a bit, and you feel up to it, come up to London and I'll treat you to an expensive haircut.'

'Any haircut would be an improvement on this,' said Kate glumly. 'But I can't do anything about it until I heal up.'

Fenny eyed the healing scar on Kate's forehead, and blew out her cheeks. 'That's it. I'm never taking the car to college. If a careful driver like you can have an accident, there's no hope for someone like me.'

One of the tasks Kate set herself, as soon as she felt up to it, was the return of the brooch. This took time and infinite care before she achieved a letter that expressed her own regret at returning it and at the same time gave no offence, since Julia Cartwright was the mother of one of Kate's pupils, as well as Jack Spencer's sister.

When she received a reply Kate was able to read between the lines very easily. Julia Cartwright, it was obvious, had never had any idea of the value of the brooch. Her brother, she explained, had volunteered to buy it for her because at the moment, due to her new baby, shopping was difficult. Abby sent her love, and Tim and Jack, she went on, joined in her good wishes for Kate's speedy recovery.

Left with a great deal of time to herself for introspection, Kate soon realised that in sending Alasdair packing she'd made a mistake. Because she was missing him badly. Now she was in a more stable frame of mind it was all too obvious that she didn't have to be wildly in love with Alasdair to enjoy his company. And, whatever her heart might feel about him, her body, even in its present battered state, clamoured for a repeat of the rapture experienced in his bed. Depressed, because this would never happen again, she steeled herself to complete silence on his part. Then on her first day downstairs she received a sheaf of bronze and gold tulips. 'From Alasdair' stated the card.

No love, or best wishes, or even a get well message. Those were the greetings which came with other flowers, from Phil and Toby and her colleagues in Foychurch, from friends and neighbours all anxious to wish her well. Downstairs the house was full of flowers everywhere in every possible container Frances could find, but Alasdair's tulips went up into Kate's bedroom—a circumstance her family nobly refrained from mentioning.

The tulips were only the first of Alasdair's offerings. Soon afterwards Kate received a parcel of brand-new books straight from the bestseller list, followed only days later by a selection of new releases on video to play on the VCR in her bedroom. Kate wrote brief, friendly notes of thanks after each arrival, secretly deeply touched by Alasdair's efforts to improve her convalescence. But eventually she gave up hoping he would visit her, and in darker moments even wondered if he'd sent the gifts to assuage his guilt over the accident. If so the guilt was unnecessary, she thought moodily. He'd rung that night out of anxiety for her. It was sheer bad luck he'd chosen the worst possible moment to do it.

When the next parcel arrived Kate opened the large box with anticipation.

'What has Alasdair sent you this time?' asked Frances.

Kate stared blankly into the box after she'd removed the plastic chippings inside. 'Wow,' she said faintly. 'It's a DVD player.'

She took a card from the envelope inside and sat down abruptly.

'We hope this is more to your taste than jewellery,' said the message. 'With best wishes from Julia, Tim, Abby, Baby John and Jack.'

Frances leaned over Kate's shoulder to look. 'Heavens above,' she said, sighing. 'You certainly started something the evening you took that child home with you.'

'I really can't send this back as well,' said Kate, frowning.

'Of course not. Just send a note of graceful but restrained thanks.' Frances paused. 'Do you think this is Mr Spencer's doing, too?'

'I don't know. I'll address my thanks to them all in general.' Kate smiled. 'You don't have to worry, Mother. Jack Spencer's a very nice man, with no dark, ulterior motive, I promise. He's not on an intellectual level with Alasdair, maybe, and certainly not as well off. But I can enjoy his company even so, just as I do with Phil and Toby.'

'Just good friends,' said her mother, resigned. 'Which is certainly not what Julian would settle for.'

'Or Alasdair,' said Kate tartly.

'You'd never guess!'

Alasdair broke his silence eventually by ringing Kate one evening after she'd taken herself off to her room to watch one of his videos on her old VCR.

'How are you?' he asked.

'Improving. How are you?'

'Busy.'

'How's the job?'

'Demanding.'

Silence for a moment.

'What were you doing when I rang?' he asked.

'Watching one of videos you sent. You've been very

kind, Alasdair, and I appreciate the gifts. They were thoughtful. But I'm not an invalid now. You don't have to send me any more.'

'As you wish. Did you post the brooch back?'

'Yes. By the tone of her answering letter Mrs Cartwright obviously had no idea of its value.' Kate paused. 'She sent me something else instead—a DVD player.'

'A DVD player,' he repeated. 'Spencer's idea again?'

'The card said the gift came from the entire family, Jack included. And I can hardly send it back this time. Not that it's much use to me at present. I don't have anything to play on it—' The moment the words were out Kate could have bitten her tongue. 'But I'm going to hire something from the local video shop tomorrow,' she added hastily, relieved when she heard a slight, but distinct chuckle from him.

'Riveting subject though he is, let's forget Jack Spencer and his family for the moment. There's something I need to say.'

Kate waited, hardly daring to breathe.

'Are you still there?' he demanded.

'Yes.'

'Kate, if you ever change your mind the offer's still on the table. You need only say the word.'

She let out the breath she'd been holding. 'Thank you, Alasdair. But nothing's changed.'

There was silence for a moment. 'I'd like to come and see you, Kate, just the same.'

No way, thought Kate in panic. Having gone this far without seeing him, she wanted—*needed*—to look a whole lot more appealing before they met again. 'Alasdair, please don't be offended—'

'But you don't want that,' he finished for her. 'Right. Sorry I suggested it.'

'Alasdair, you don't understand!'

'I understand only too well,' he said bitterly. 'Goodbye, Kate.'

She was depressed for days after the call and fully expected silence from Alasdair afterwards, but as time went by he rang occasionally, though there was no more talk of visiting her, nor a renewal of his offer. Instead he talked about his job and the progress on his house. They chatted about the approaching Easter holidays, and the family reunion expected at Friars Wood, and Kate expressed pleasure she was far from feeling when Alasdair informed her he was flying to New York.

Not, she assured herself afterwards, that she had the least right to feel jealous. What Alasdair did during the Easter break—even if he was doing it with Amy again—was nothing to do with her. But, in love with him or not, the thought of him in bed with another woman cut her to pieces. Disgusted with herself, she thrust the thought away and reminded herself that after the holiday she would be going back to Foychurch and her job, and life could get back to normal.

Before the holiday Kate took a trip to London to stay with Leo and Jonah, and let them to treat her to a frighteningly expensive haircut which did wonders for her morale. Now it had grown a little the genius with the scissors was able to transform her ragged mop into feathery curls, some of which fell in a half-fringe across her forehead to hide one scar. The rest, he assured her, would soon be long enough to curl on the back of her neck to hide the other.

The sum Leo handed over for the transformation took Kate's breath away, but her sister told her it was worth every penny to see her smile at her reflection again. Kate was passionately grateful for the boost to her self-confidence. When everyone was together at Friars Wood over Easter she would be able to enjoy the occasion far more now she was looking more normal. Different, but definitely normal.

When Kate returned to Foychurch a couple of days before term started she stopped dead when she opened her cottage door. The room was full of flowers, so many that some of them were in containers which didn't belong to her. She went straight round to Mr Reith, who greeted her with affection and told her the flowers had been delivered earlier and, not knowing how late she would be, he'd put them in water in anything he could find, including some vases of his own. He told her she looked pretty as a picture with her new haircut, expressed his deep relief at her recovery, and handed her the card that had come with the flowers.

Back in her cottage Kate opened the envelope eagerly, but the welcome home message was from Jack Spencer, not Alasdair. Something she'd known, in her heart of hearts. Alasdair would never have sent such a vast profusion of flowers.

It was late that evening when Kate finally made supper from the various supplies Frances had packed into her new car. This was a second-hand model, a different make from her old one, but similar enough to feel familiar when she'd begun driving again. The first day out in it had been a nerve-racking experience. Before the accident driving had been like breathing, something she did without thinking, but now Kate found she had to drive every inch of the way with fierce concentration, and today's journey had left her so limp with fatigue she'd needed a long, relaxing soak in a bath with a book before even thinking of food.

Someone knocked on her front door when she was about to eat her meal from a tray on the sofa, and Kate jumped up eagerly to answer it. But instead of Alasdair, as she'd so desperately hoped, she found Jack Spencer on her doorstep, in formal dark suit, looking taken aback at the sight of her.

'Hello, Kate. You were obviously expecting someone else.'

She pulled herself together hurriedly. 'No, not at all. Do come in.'

'How are you?' he asked.

'Almost as good as new. Thank you so much for the flowers.'

'My pleasure. Your brother told me you were getting back today,' he said, the familiar smile firmly back in place, but his eyes still on her hair.

'I arrived a couple of hours ago. In time to get myself together for a day or two before starting work. I'm just having a lazy supper in front of the TV.'

'And I'm interrupting it,' he apologised, 'so I'll get to the point. Have dinner with me one night to celebrate your recovery?'

Kate looked at him thoughtfully. Jack Spencer was a likeable, attractive man. But the flowers and the extravagant presents, and his visits to the hospital, probably meant he wanted some kind of relationship with her. And this was out of the question. She searched for a way to refuse without giving offence and smiled wryly when she saw he was still fascinated by her hair.

'You look so different, Kate. New hairdo. What made you cut it all off?'

'They had to chop it off at the hospital.'

He grimaced. 'God, you were so lucky! What actually happened?'

She gave him a brief account of the accident, then expressed her thanks again, to him and to his family, for the DVD player.

'Our pleasure.' he smiled sheepishly. 'I obviously made a mistake, big time, with the brooch.'

'I thought it came from your sister,' said Kate quickly, and he shrugged.

'She wasn't up to shopping at the time, so I got it for her at Dysart's when I went to the auction, as you probably know.'

'I do. And how much it cost. Which is why I sent it back.'

He nodded. 'Jules gave me a right old lecture about it. So I thought up the DVD player instead.'

Be blunt, she told herself. 'If it had come first I would have returned that, too, but I just couldn't do it a second time.' She looked him in the eye. 'I did very little to deserve it, Jack. It was embarrassing.'

'It wasn't meant to be!'

'I know. Which is why I kept it. And your sister is the mother of one of my pupils, so I had no choice.'

'Never mind Julia.' He perched on the window seat, obviously prepared to stay, and with a feeling of resignation Kate sat down on the sofa. 'Let's talk about why you object to gifts from me, Kate.'

'Is this just about you, then?' asked Kate. 'I thought the gift came from the whole family.'

'It did—'

'But you paid for it?'

He shrugged. 'I plead guilty on that one.'

'And to posing as my fiancé to visit me in the hospital? Might as well get it all in the open at once.'

He grinned sheepishly. 'I admit I sort of implied it to one of the nurses, so I could sneak in to see you. But I didn't know then that you'd lost your memory, Kate. You must know I wouldn't harm a hair of your head—' He bit his lip, and she smiled.

'Don't worry. I won't throw a wobbly if you mention hair.' Kate felt sudden remorse. 'If I've been rude I apologise,' she began, but Jack held up a large, capable hand.

'No, you haven't. I'm the one who's overstepped the mark, and I'm sorry. Put it down to a lack of finesse. When I want something I tend to go for it hell for leather.'

'If you mean you want some kind of relationship with me,' she said gently, 'I'm afraid that's not on.'

His mouth twisted. 'Because of your friend Drummond?'

'He has nothing to do with it,' she said untruthfully. 'I just believe in being honest.' And Jack, she could see, wasn't enjoying her candour any more than Alasdair had.

'So what's the problem? Do you actively dislike me? Or is it just that I'm lacking in the intellect department?' he demanded.

'Your intellect seems in pretty good shape to me.' Kate smiled at him to soften the blow. 'I like you very much, Jack. But—'

'No buts,' he said quickly, and gave her a wry grin. 'No need to fill in the blanks, Kate. I understand.'

She smiled gratefully, then looked at her meal waiting on the tray. 'Look, have you eaten? I can soon rustle up some supper.'

He jumped up immediately, shaking his head. 'I didn't come here for that, Kate.'

'I know. But if you'll settle for salad and a wedge of

my mother's bacon and egg pie you're more than welcome,' she assured him.

Jack looked at her thoughtfully for a moment, then
nodded. 'Thank you, I will. I'd be a fool to turn down
the only meal I'll ever share with you.'

Once she'd provided Jack with a hefty slice of the pie
Frances had made because it was her daughter's favourite comfort food, Kate resumed her own meal. Now the
air was cleared, and she felt he wouldn't misinterpret her
interest, she asked Jack about his cottage.

He described the restoration work he was doing on it,
talking with enthusiasm, until a peremptory knock on
Kate's front door called a halt to the conversation. Her
heart leapt, then sank like a stone as she opened the door
to a very cold, hostile Alasdair Drummond.

CHAPTER TWELVE

'ALASDAIR!' she said brightly. 'What a surprise.'

'So I see. Good evening, Kate,' he said formally, throwing a glance like a steel blade at Jack. 'Adam said you'd be back here today. How are you feeling?'

'A lot better,' Kate informed him wishing she were anywhere else on the planet. 'Please come in. Would you like some coffee? You know Jack Spencer, of course.'

The two men nodded coolly.

'No coffee, thanks,' said Alasdair. 'It was just a flying visit, Kate. If your lights had been out I wouldn't have disturbed you as late as this.'

'It's only just after ten,' she said tartly.

'Look, I should be going,' said Jack uneasily, looking from one face to the other.

'Not on my account,' said Alasdair, giving him a glacial look. 'I'm the intruder. Glad to see you looking so much better, Kate. I'll ring you some time.' He gave her a smile which froze her blood, turned on his heel and strode down the path to his car.

Kate stared after him in anguish for a moment, then shut the door, resisting the urge to lean against it, movie-style, as she smiled at Jack. 'Sorry about that.'

His answering grin was wry. 'Not as sorry as me. I shouldn't have been here. Your friend didn't like it at all.'

'Who I invite to my house is absolutely nothing to do with Alasdair,' she assured him.

'Try telling him that!' His mouth went down at the corners. 'Besides, you didn't invite me, Kate. I barged in, as usual.'

'So did Alasdair.'

'For a moment I thought he was going to knock me cold—he certainly wanted to!'

Kate pulled a face. 'I'm glad he didn't. You wouldn't have stood by and let him, and my cottage is too small for brawling.'

Jack eyed her with remorse. 'Your friend was not at all happy to find me here. Jealous as hell, in fact.'

Kate felt a rush of ignoble satisfaction. 'He has no right to be.'

'Are you in love with him?'

'Good heavens, no. We're friends, that's all. From way back.'

'Miss Dysart,' Jack said indulgently, 'who are you trying to kid?'

'I'm fond of Alasdair,' she said, colouring. 'But that's all.'

'If you say so,' he said, grinning. 'But believe me, Kate, his feelings are a lot warmer than that. The guy wanted to floor me, then carry you off over his shoulder.'

Kate shook her head, laughing. 'No way! Alasdair's not that kind—'

'All men are that kind,' he assured her, then held out his hand. 'Thank you for supper, Kate. I hope we meet again some time.'

'So do I,' she said, with such sincerity he leaned forward and kissed her cheek.

'Take care, Kate.'

Kate opened the door for him, then peered out into the darkness. 'Where's your car?'

Jack winked. 'I parked it down the lane out of sight, to preserve your reputation!'

Kate laughed, wished him goodnight, then shut her door again and locked it this time, her mind working overtime. Alasdair had said he was in the neighbourhood, but Foychurch was pretty much off the beaten track. He'd looked weary enough to be on his way home from work. Unless the haggard look was the result of jet lag. Or sex with Amy.

For various reasons, Kate did not go happy to bed.

Kate was given a warm welcome when she started back at school, from staff and children alike. Touched to receive posies of flowers and little gifts from her class, she thanked them all for her wonderful get well card, relieved when Abby smiled shyly but came giftless. Once lessons got underway Kate noticed that the child seemed a lot happier in class, and later felt pleased when she saw that Abby was part of a noisy gang in the playground.

At the end of the week Abby came running back in after school. 'I usually go home with Bethany's mother, Miss Dysart, but Mummy's come for me today, with the baby,' she said breathlessly. 'She asked if you could spare a minute to talk to her.'

'Miss Dysart, how pretty you look with short hair,' Julia Cartwright exclaimed when Kate joined her at the car. 'Sorry to drag you out, but I couldn't leave the baby.'

Kate peered in at the chubby baby boy asleep in his car seat, and smiled at Abby. 'He's beautiful—and looks just like you!'

The child smiled with pleasure, then got in beside the baby as Julia took Kate aside. 'How are you feeling?

Abby was utterly beside herself when we heard what happened. She was so sure you were dead Jack insisted on taking her to the hospital to see you. I hope you didn't mind.'

'Of course not. Abby seems a lot happier these days. More integrated into the class.'

'Once she knew you were all right she began to settle down, oddly enough.' Julia hesitated. 'My brother's gone back to London, by the way. He's been playing hookey a bit lately.'

'London?' said Kate, surprised. 'I thought his cottage wasn't far from here.'

'It isn't. It's near Hereford. But that's just a weekend retreat. Jack's actual home is in London, near his head office.'

Head office?

'He's been down this way for a while lately, to hold interviews and start up the Hereford office, which Tim is going to run.' Julia smiled. 'The firm was Jack's baby when it started, but it's grown a bit since then. Aspen Homes is quite a success story for the boy who started on a pittance as a hod-carrier.'

Aspen Homes, thought Kate stunned. The company that built everything from modest homes for first-time buyers to expensive waterfront developments. 'He never mentioned that.'

'I thought not.' Julia smiled. 'I came to say I quite understand about the brooch. To be honest, I would have sent you a camellia in a pot instead. But when Jack insisted on the DVD player I hadn't the heart to say no. For a hard-headed businessman he's very generous to people he likes.'

Kate smiled awkwardly. 'Thank you for explaining. I had no idea.'

'Well, you wouldn't from Jack,' said his sister. 'I think he was rather hoping you'd like him for himself.'

'I do, Mrs Cartwright. But only as a friend.'

Julia nodded. 'Pity. Jack would make someone a wonderful husband.'

Kate was very thoughtful that night. Instead of willing Alasdair to ring, the same as every other night since the debacle of her first evening home, she gave some thought to Jack Spencer and everything he'd achieved from his beginnings as hod-carrier to his present spectacular success. Any other man would have used the story, and his financial standing, to gain his ends, but not Jack. Kate heaved a sigh. She liked Jack a lot. But his one great drawback was the fact that he wasn't Alasdair.

Kate slumped down on the sofa as she admitted the truth at last. Now Alasdair had come back into her life she wanted him to stay in it. Preferably forever. But to let him know that she needed to see him face to face.

It was something Kate longed for more and more as time went by without a word from him. The days went past quickly enough once she was back in the school routine. Often when there were extra-curricular calls on her time it was early evening or later before she got home, and for the time being the job took all her depleted energies. She had even given up her role in the dramatic society's forthcoming production of *An Ideal Husband*, so that evenings once given over to rehearsals could now be spent in the same way as all her other evenings. Waiting for Alasdair to ring.

But two weeks after Alasdair's ill-fated appearance on her doorstep Kate resigned herself to the fact that he was never going to ring. And she had no intention of ringing End House. The danger of his hostile Edinburgh-tinged

tones telling her to get lost was far too great. So there
was only one thing for it. She would just have to pocket
her pride and go to End House this weekend to see him
in person. However hard he worked during the week,
Alasdair must surely take Sunday off.

By Friday afternoon Kate was sorry she'd decided on
Sunday. It meant she had a whole school-free Saturday
to get through beforehand. So when Ally Ferris, who
taught the nursery class, suggested lunch in Hereford
next day, with a trip to the cinema afterwards, Kate
agreed with enthusiasm, grateful to pass the time so
pleasantly.

It was late in the evening when she got home, and,
after the usual disappointment when she found no message on her phone from Alasdair, Kate had a chat with
her mother to report on her health, went to bed early
with a book she'd bought, and did a lot of hard thinking
about whether the visit to Alasdair was a good idea after
all. But if she didn't make the effort she'd go mad, Kate
decided at last. Even though there was always the possibility that he wouldn't be there, even if she did drive
to End House. He could be away for the weekend, or
even on a trip back to New York for all she knew.

After a week of heavy showers and very few bright
periods, Sunday dawned sunny and even warm, Kate
found when she ventured out into the garden to put more
nuts out for the birds and to chat over the hedge with
Mr Reith, who was doing some weeding. So later, aban-
doning winter wool for a white shirt and the coral trousers her mother had bought for her, Kate tossed her
windbreaker in the car and set off for Gloucester.

Her hair had grown a little, the fringe now long
enough to brush one eyebrow and the hair at the back
curling very satisfactorily to disguise the scar on her

neck. And because it was daytime, and sunny, and the bruises were long gone, Kate left her face pretty much to itself, other than a touch of mascara and lipstick. She was confident she looked rather good today. And hoped Alasdair would be in agreement. Though there was always the possibility that he'd slam his door shut the moment he saw her face.

Kate thrust the thought away, and concentrated on her driving. And eventually, even though she drove as slowly as safety allowed, and stopped *en route* for coffee and a Sunday paper, she finally reached End House.

Kate had no problem with space to park, because there was no sign of Alasdair's car. So it was worst-case scenario after all. He wasn't here. She got out of the car and rang the bell, just in case. No response. She peered through the large bay window into the drawing room, then through its twin into the dining room. But no Alasdair. Kate went round the house to look in at the kitchen window. Still no sign of him. Short of acquiring a ladder, there was no way she could look into the bedroom windows, and if Alasdair was up there in bed he wasn't answering the doorbell.

Kate got back in the car, deflated. Perhaps he'd gone out for a paper or something. In which case she would wait for a bit. Because she'd never have the nerve for this again. She sat reading the paper for a while, but the words on the page made so little sense that at last she gave up and faced facts. Alasdair could be out for the day, so she might as well go home.

She switched on the engine, backed round the lawn and drove towards the entrance—then gasped in horror and slammed on her brakes to avoid collision with a vehicle coming the other way. There was a tooth-grinding crunch as her car made contact with one of the stone gateposts, and Kate, appalled but unhurt, switched off the engine and released her seat belt as Alasdair burst from the other car and came to wrench her door open.

'*Kate!* Are you hurt?' he demanded.

'No. Just horribly embarrassed,' she assured him, her face as red as her new trousers. 'When I saw you I couldn't pull up in time.' She tried to smile. 'I hope my insurance will be kind. It's not long since I wrote off another car—'

'Shut up!' snapped Alasdair. 'Do you think I'd forgotten that?' He pulled her out of the car and looked her up and down. 'You appear to be in one piece,' he commented, his voice so wintry she shrivelled up inside.

'Yes, thank you.' Kate thought of trying a winning smile, but Alasdair's eyes were so cold she abandoned the idea, and watched in suspense as he bent to examine her car.

'Get in and back away,' ordered Alasdair.

Kate slid into the driving seat, switched on the ignition and began to reverse, then stopped dead. She wound down her window and looked at Alasdair in horror. 'What was that horrible noise?'

'Your bumper. It's dragging. Keep reversing while I get rid of this broken glass.'

Every tooth on edge at the noise, Kate did as he said, parked, then sat behind the wheel while Alasdair fetched a garden broom and did some sweeping up. Afterwards he drove in to park beside her, then got out, motioning her to do the same. They stood together in silence, examining the damage to her car, which had a dent in the bonnet and a mangled bumper. The broken glass had formerly been one of the headlights.

'You can't drive back in that,' he said brusquely.

'Can't you just tie the bumper back on, or something?' she asked hopefully.

'No. Nor do I happen to have a replacement headlight.' Alasdair motioned her towards the house. 'Come inside. You look shaken.'

'Understandable,' she snapped. 'It's not long since the accident, remember?'

He gave her a glare. 'So you keep reminding me!'

'Anyway, it's not my fault. You should have a mirror fixed in the lane outside your gate,' said Kate, furious with herself for ever thinking it was a good idea to come here. 'I had no idea you were driving in at that moment.'

'I happen to live here,' he said tersely, unlocking the door.

Kate stalked inside, her head in the air, wondering how on earth she was to get home. 'Are there any garages around who would do a repair?' she asked, as he led the way to the kitchen.

'On a Sunday?' He shot her a scathing look. 'I doubt it. Sit down. I'll make some coffee.'

Kate was very glad to sit down. Now she had attention to spare for them she realised her knees were trembling. She pulled on her sweater, even though the kitchen seemed even warmer than before now the walls were painted in one of the soft shades of red she'd suggested. She wanted to tell Alasdair that, but decided not to. If there was any talking to be done he must start the ball rolling.

When they were facing each other over steaming mugs of coffee, the fragrance brought back memories of their last night here so vividly Kate choked on the first sip.

'Too hot?' he asked. 'Would you like more milk?'

She shook her head dumbly, cursing herself for coming here to End House. There was no point now in telling Alasdair she'd changed her mind. His offer was obviously no longer open.

'I'm so sorry,' she said belatedly.

'What for, exactly?' he enquired.

Kate glared at him. 'For smashing into your gatepost, of course! Naturally I'll pay for the damage—'

'Don't be stupid,' he snapped, his eyes fixed on hers with unnerving intensity. 'To hell with the gatepost. Why are you here, Kate?'

Good question. Right now she couldn't think of one good reason for being in Alasdair Drummond's granite-faced company.

'It's a nice day, and I fancied a drive,' she said shortly.

'And you just happened to be passing End House?'

She looked away, not even bothering to reply.

There was silence for a moment while Alasdair kept the unnerving grey gaze on her face. 'You look well, Kate. Are you?'

'I'm fine.'

'Good.'

This was torture. Kate drank her coffee down, and looked at him in appeal. 'If I leave the car here could you get someone to repair it?'

'Certainly.'

It was like drawing blood from a stone. She took her phone from her bag. 'Then if I could have your telephone directory I'll ring for a taxi to take me back to Foychurch.'

'No need for that. I'll drive you back.'

Kate looked up to surprise a gleam in the grey eyes before he schooled them to impassivity again. The wretch was actually enjoying her misery! 'I couldn't possibly let you do that,' she said with hauteur, then had a depressing thought. Taxi drivers liked cash.

'What now?' he asked.

'I'm afraid I need a lift to a bank,' she said reluctantly.

'Why?'

'I don't have enough cash for a taxi.'

'You could borrow some from me.'

She'd walk home first. 'No, thanks. A lift to a bank would do.' Her eyes clashed with him. 'Or you could just give me directions to one and I'll walk there.'

'Don't be silly,' said Alasdair for the second time, in a tone which made Kate burn to hit him. 'I'll get your car repaired tomorrow and I'll drive you back to Foychurch later today. On one condition.'

'What is it?' she said suspiciously.

'That you tell me why you're here.'

She looked at him in silence while she thought up various lies.

'The truth, Kate,' he said sternly.

She sighed deeply. 'Oh, all right, Alasdair. Last time we met you went off in a huff. I thought I'd come and mend fences.' Her chin lifted. 'It wasn't an easy thing to do.'

'You find driving hard since the accident?'

'As it happens, I do. But that's not what I meant.'

'I know.' His eyes held hers. 'So what would have happened if I hadn't turned up at that moment?'

Kate shrugged. 'I would have driven home.'

'Are you with Jack Spencer now?' he said conversationally.

She gave him a scathing look. 'I wouldn't be here today if I were. He's gone back to London. He builds a lot more houses than I thought, by the way. He's the brains behind Aspen Homes.'

'I know. I did some research about him.'

'Why?'

Alasdair's mouth twisted. 'To make sure he was good enough for you, Kate. When I found Spencer with you that night, I assumed he'd won at last. God knows he'd tried hard enough.'

'It was quite the reverse, actually,' said Kate, glad that she sounded so calm. 'I'd just told him there was no possibility of a relationship between us.'

'So why the devil didn't you let me know that?' he said with sudden violence. 'When I found out he was worth millions, I assumed—'

'You assumed what, exactly?' she spat in fury. 'That I'd pounced on him the minute I knew he was rich? Thanks a lot.' She pushed back her chair with a screech on the stone flags and jumped up to make for the door, but Alasdair leapt to catch her and pulled her round to face him.

'How would you have felt?' he flung at her, his hands biting into her arms. 'He was there, on your sofa, the room so full of bloody flowers they had to be from him, and you'd obviously just shared a meal. What the hell was I supposed to think? You'd thrown my ring back in my face—'

'I didn't throw it—'

'Don't split hairs!'

Kate looked down at the fingers that were gripping her so hard the knuckles were white. 'You're hurting me, Alasdair.'

He dropped his hands and moved back. 'Right. Let's get things straight. You don't want Jack Spencer, you don't want me, so what the hell do you want, Kate? The moon?'

'No.' She looked up into his angry face, and rubbed

her arms. Oh, well, now or never. 'I—I want to know if you still mean the things you said last time I was here,' she said in a rush.

He was silent so long Kate's eyes fell to hide her despair.

'Yes,' he said at last, an odd note in his voice. 'I still mean them.'

Relief made Kate giddy. 'I hoped you did,' she said gruffly.

Alasdair caught her in his arms. 'What are you saying, Kate?'

She leaned against him, feeling the thud of his heart through his sweater, and shivered at the thought of what she might have lost by being too pig-headed to face the truth. That she loved Alasdair. Always had. Always would.

'You're cold, darling,' said Alasdair huskily, and took her by the hand to hurry her into the small sitting room he'd made into a study since her last time here. He scooped her up and sat down with her in his lap. 'Now, tell me what you mean. Exactly.'

'I wasn't lying, Alasdair. I'd convinced myself I was over you.' She smiled wryly. 'After you made love to me I knew very well that I wasn't. But I still wouldn't give in. Pride, I suppose. Then I had the accident, and you were so shocked at the sight of my hair the same pride made me push you away.'

'All that mattered to me was that you were alive. I didn't care a damn about the hair,' he said fiercely, and kissed her at last, and she responded so fiercely he went on kissing her until neither of them could breathe. 'So why did you keep me away?' he demanded at last.

'Pure vanity, Alasdair,' she said breathlessly, and buried her face against his shoulder. 'I wanted—needed—

to wait until I was less of a fright to look at. I was going to invite you to Friars Wood over Easter, once I'd had my hair done in London. But you went to New York to see Amy instead.'

He put an ungentle hand under her chin and jerked her face up to his. 'I went to the States for meetings at Healthshield,' he said, and kissed her roughly. 'I had no intention of seeing Amy.'

Kate kissed him back. 'I was so jealous, Alasdair. I couldn't sleep for thinking of you making love to her!'

'I'm glad. I hope you suffered the way I did when I found you with Spencer!' He shook her a little, then frowned. 'Which reminds me. There was no sign of his Cherokee that night. If there had been I'd have gone straight home again.'

Kate gave a little gurgle of laughter. 'He parked it somewhere else to preserve the schoolmarm's reputation!' She sobered suddenly. 'But you should be grateful he came to see me that night. I watched you storm off down the path and out of my life, as I thought. And when the subject of a relationship with Jack came up the penny dropped at last. This famous brain of mine finally solved the equation. There was no hope for Jack for the simple reason that he wasn't you, Alasdair.'

He crushed her close, and suddenly all the pent-up feelings of the past few weeks overwhelmed them simultaneously. They slid to the floor, too desperate for each other to waste time in finding a bed. The first time they'd made love Alasdair had played her like an instrument until they made music together. This time there was no thought for either of them beyond the basic need to come together in a passionate celebration of love and need and ultimate, gasping rapture, and when, all to

soon, their short, sweet mating was over Alasdair held
her close as their breathing slowed.

'Does this mean you'll marry me?' he demanded,
when he could speak.

Kate shook her head, glorying in the shock in his eyes
before she relented. 'One day. But not yet. You have to
come a-courting for a while first, Mr Drummond.'

'Witch!' He shook her a little. 'Whatever you say. But
don't make me wait too long, darling.'

Kate gave a wry glance at their scattered clothes. 'I
didn't make you wait at all.'

'I didn't give you the chance!' Alasdair laughed, and
ruffled her hair. 'I like the new haircut, by the way,' he
said, kissing the fading scar on her forehead. 'You look
delicious.'

'I'm glad you think so.' So glad she hugged him con-
vulsively.

'Stay with me tonight,' he commanded. 'I'll drive you
back in the morning, in good time for school.'

Kate nodded happily. 'I can't go until you drive me
anyway, so I'm in your hands.'

'Damn right you are,' said Alasdair promptly, 'and
from now on, physically or metaphorically, that's where
you're going to stay.'

'Forever and ever, amen,' she agreed. 'Where were
you this morning, by the way?'

He hesitated, then his lips twitched and he began to
laugh. 'I went to Foychurch.'

Kate stared incredulously for a moment, then dissolved into laughter with him. 'You mean we passed
each other on the way?' she gasped at last.

'Must have. I drove back like a bat out of hell, then
lost ten years of my life when you hit that gatepost.'

'Why were you in such a hurry to get back?'

'Because your neighbour said you'd gone to Gloucester. Of course I was in a hurry!' Alasdair kissed her, and she kissed him back for a blissful moment then pushed him away.

'But why did you wait so *long* before coming to Foychurch?' she demanded wrathfully. 'I've been miserable.'

'I'm glad to hear it. So have I.' His eyes lit with a wry gleam. 'If you want the truth, Katharine Dysart, the chauvinist in me wanted you to come to me first.'

She gave him the kind of shove usually reserved for Adam. 'Which I did, Alasdair Drummond!'

He shook his head. 'No, you didn't. I caved in first. I drove over to see you yesterday. But you were out.'

Kate's eyes rounded with surprise. 'You came yesterday, too? Why didn't you ring first?'

'A question I asked myself when I found the bird had flown again today! But I needed to see you face to face, Kate, not talk on the phone.' He smiled crookedly. 'I had this really mature idea about throwing you over my shoulder and making off with you if you were difficult again.'

She smiled smugly. 'Jack was right, then. He said you wanted to the night you stormed out of my cottage.'

Alasdair looked dangerous for a moment. 'Forget about Jack Spencer,' he ordered, 'and concentrate on me from now on!'

She nodded. 'OK. Can I have the ring back, then?'

'No, you can't. I returned it.'

Kate stared at him in such dismay Alasdair grinned.

'You can choose another as soon as we can get to a jeweller. After you turned it down I took a dislike to that one.'

'Good. I'm not keen on diamonds.'

'Neither am I, now.' He pulled her to her feet. 'Come on. Time for breakfast.'

'Haven't you had anything to eat yet?'

Alasdair smiled. 'I was in too much of a hurry to get to you.'

'Then you really love me! When a man puts a woman before food he must be serious.'

'Damn right I'm serious,' Alasdair assured her. 'Now let's eat.'

'Fine by me,' said Kate, then her heart skipped a beat at the smile he gave her.

'What shall we do for the rest of the day?' asked Alasdair. 'Read the Sunday papers, take a trip to the cinema?'

Kate shook her head. 'I read *my* paper while I was waiting in my car for you, and I went to the cinema yesterday. So let's just stay home and watch television. You must have bought a set by now?' she added hopefully.

'I certainly have.' His eyes gleamed suggestively. 'But it's in my bedroom.'

Kate received the news with such unashamed delight Alasdair caught her close, kissing her with a passion she returned in full measure. Held so tightly she couldn't breathe, she managed to free her mouth for a second to tell him something important. 'Alasdair,' she gasped, 'I think maybe I could wait a while for breakfast.'

His eyes gleamed. 'You mean you want to watch TV?'

'You know exactly what I want!'

'First,' he said sternly, 'you have to tell me you love me.'

Kate took in a deep breath and looked deep into his

demanding eyes. 'Of course I love you, Alasdair Drummond. I always did. I always will.'

Alasdair let out his own breath and rubbed his cheek against hers. 'For that, my darling, you get breakfast in bed later. If you're good,' he added huskily.

'I'm always good.' She batted her eyelashes at him. 'But with a bit more coaching I could be fantastic!'

The world's bestselling romance series.

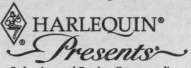

HARLEQUIN®
Presents

Seduction and Passion Guaranteed!

We are pleased to announce
Sandra Marton's fantastic new series

The O'CONNELLS

In order to marry, they've got to gamble on love!

Don't miss...

KEIR O'CONNELL'S MISTRESS

Keir O'Connell knew it was time to leave Las Vegas when he became
consumed with desire for a dancer. The heat of the desert must have
addled his brain! He headed east and set himself up in business—
but thoughts of the dancing girl wouldn't leave his head.
And then one day there she was, Cassie...

Harlequin Presents #2309
On sale March 2003

Pick up a Harlequin Presents® novel and you will enter a world
of spine-tingling passion and provocative, tantalizing romance!

Available wherever Harlequin books are sold.

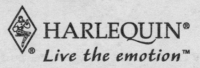

HARLEQUIN®
Live the emotion™

Visit us at www.eHarlequin.com

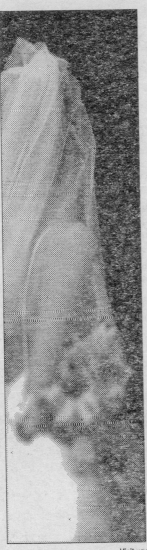

The world's bestselling romance series.

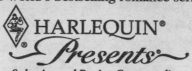

HARLEQUIN®
Presents

Seduction and Passion Guaranteed!

INTERNATIONAL
DOCTORS

They're guaranteed to raise your pulse!

**Meet the most eligible medical men of the world,
in a new series of stories, by popular authors,
that will make your heart race!**

**Whether they're saving lives or dealing with desire,
our doctors have got bedside manners that
send temperatures soaring....**

Coming in Harlequin Presents in 2003:

THE DOCTOR'S SECRET CHILD by Catherine Spencer
#2311, on sale March

THE PASSION TREATMENT by Kim Lawrence
#2330, on sale June

THE DOCTOR'S RUNAWAY BRIDE by Sarah Morgan
#2366, on sale December

**Pick up a Harlequin Presents® novel and you will enter a world
of spine-tingling passion and provocative, tantalizing romance!**

Available wherever Harlequin books are sold.

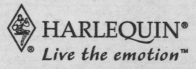

HARLEQUIN®
Live the emotion™

Visit us at www.eHarlequin.com

HPINTDOC

If you enjoyed what you just read,
then we've got an offer you can't resist!

Take 2 bestselling
love stories FREE!
Plus get a FREE surprise gift!

The world's bestselling romance series.

HARLEQUIN® *Presents*

Seduction and Passion Guaranteed!

Hot-Blooded Husbands

Let them keep you warm tonight!

Don't miss the final part of Michelle Reid's red-hot series!

A PASSIONATE MARRIAGE

Greek tycoon Leandros Petronades married Isobel on the crest of a wild affair. But within a year the marriage crashed and burned. Three years later, Leandros wants to finalize their divorce—or thinks he does. But face-to-face with Isobel again, he finds their all-consuming mutual attraction is as strong as ever....

Harlequin Presents #2307
On sale March 2003

Pick up a Harlequin Presents® novel and you will enter a world of spine-tingling passion and provocative, tantalizing romance!

Available wherever Harlequin books are sold.

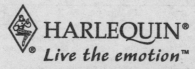

HARLEQUIN®
Live the emotion™

Visit us at www.eHarlequin.com